CONTENTS

DEDICATION

CHAPTER

DEDICATION

I dedicate this book to my father, Arthur, who, at the present time, is struggling through old age himself. My hope is that this story amuses him somewhat and, perhaps, even inspires him to cope with the process of aging just a little bit better.

CHAPTER 1

GOODBYES AND REGRETS

Sandra kisses me gently on the cheek. My skin feels surprisingly soft to her. I think she expected a slightly different sensation seeing as the rest of me appears so wrinkled. I look like one of those crumpled up pieces of paper her daddy casts away after a letter writing campaign has gone awry.

I squeeze her tightly and hold her for a few lasting seconds trying to stretch it out for as long as possible. I know that this could be the last time. I might not have another chance. I soak up the love the little lady so eagerly surrenders. She will be seven next July. The last six or seven years have gone by so quickly. It seems like only yesterday little Sandy took her first steps and learned her first words. I remember the night I received the telephone call and how Brian's voice on the other end of the line trembled overcome by joy as he informed me that I now had a granddaughter- all six and a half pounds of her. The next morning I saw and held her for the first time, feeling in my hands the newness of youth, and I felt the sense of accomplishment and purpose that came with knowing part of me would endure on into future generations. I felt as if I were almost young again.

That sensation rushes over me once again as I stand here holding my little granddaughter under the chalk grey skies that so often come to dominate late November. The cold wind rustles Sandra's hair and numbs my fingers. The circulation in my hands isn't what it used to be. It isn't even what it was six and a half years ago. Now I would have a hard time trying to hold a baby for fear of dropping her. A lot of things can change in seven years. Time doesn't stop for anyone or anything.

You often don't appreciate the little things in life when you are younger. The little things seem so easy that you rarely give them a second thought. It is hard not to take them for granted. There are always much more pressing issues at hand to occupy our keen young minds. But everyone ages and everyone slows down and I find that those little things, which once seemed second nature, are no longer so easily attained. I am left to wonder how I ever performed such feats of greatness, even as a younger man. When the body fails to co-operate, it is not long after that that the mind throws in with the enemy, finding it to be the most agreeable alternative.

As I release and bid farewell to what has been so dear to my heart through all these years of struggle and joy, I understand why I find myself leaving this part of the country: I can no longer stand the cold. But in spite of its coolness of climate and fondness for umbrellas and raincoats, I have still referred to it as home for the past seventy-one years. I was born here, not more than four miles from where I stand, and up until now, I expected I would die here as well.

As it turns out, it is for the sake of love that I am being forced to leave. However, I find it hard to taste bitterness in that irony because I know it is best for everyone. I can always blame the climate for its harshness and unfriendly demeanour towards the elderly, or perhaps that in itself is the thing to point notice at. Old age is the culprit whom I seek to blame. It crept up on me so slowly that at first I hardly took notice. Once I began to feel its gnawing effects, it was then too late to retreat from its clutches. So when Julie so sweetly said to me "we love you dad, and we just want you to be around forever" then Brian added with a little more suppressed enthusiasm "maybe going down south for half the year wouldn't be such a half bad idea" and "we're only thinking of your health," I found myself susceptible to such suggestions. When they put it that way, I find it difficult to put up much of an argument, for I know they are right. Whether I like the idea of leaving the people and place I love or not, it has fast become just about my only alternative. The cold and dampness has already crept its way into the confines of my armor, which has grown thin and bare from all these years of living. As I stand here now- this very moment- I can feel its workings within my chest and lungs. As the November wind hints of the forthcoming winter, I feel in my bones that I am unlikely to make it through another one. It is hard to believe that I have endured winter's icy cloak with such careless abandon some seventy times before.

Sandra waves goodbye to me. I can still, if just barely, make out her facial features as the taxi cab drives away. The dull grey-blue metallic finish catches the bright November sunlight creating a glare that reflects into Sandra's eyes and causes her to squint. The exhaust plumes outwards and upwards from the rear of the car as it moves off into the distance. As their figures grow small, I try to soothe my heartbreak by imagining their thoughts.

Sandra lets out a laugh, "That looks just like grandpa smoking his pipe."

"Yes, dear, you're quite right," says her mother squeezing her hand in hers. Julie is beginning to have regrets about encouraging me to go south for the winter. What if...? She hesitates to even think it, but the thought just won't stay out of her mind. What if something is to happen to me? Well, she might as well come right out and say it. What if I die and this is the last time she ever sees me? She hates to think of me dying alone in some strange place among strangers. She feels as though she is turning her back on the man who has given her so much. Since her mother's death ten years before, my importance in her life has only multiplied in significance. A disturbing thought comes over her: she isn't quite sure who she loves the dearest, her daughter or her father. How can she even consider loving one more than the other? Maybe she cannot. She hopes she cannot. Maybe my age and failing health are at the root of those feelings. My closeness to no longer being with her makes her weigh the value of her love for me and measure it against everything else of importance in her life. She loved her mother dearly, but when it comes to her father, her love delves into another level. It seems to run deeper. She has always been Daddy's little girl.

She bites her lip and catches herself. The tears are beginning to well up in her eyes, and she doesn't want Sandra to see her cry. She has no idea how she might never see her grandpa again. She is yet to understand the cruelness of mortality and life. Julie wants to shield her from it as long as she can. She wants to shield herself from it also. She can almost go back and remember what it was like before her own innocence was lost‒ before her faith was broken. She lived in a dreamlike world of incredible happiness where everything was possible and anything could be achieved. How that world slowly fell away over the years, level by level, as the coldness of reality became more dominant in her life. Just thinking of the place she once inhabited brings a warm feeling over her, overcoming the cold. How she wishes she could go back. Some people spend their entire life running away from their childhood. She is trying to run back towards it. If she can't do that, she is at least going to try her hardest to hang onto what slim part of it she still has. She has already made up her mind that that is not going to be taken away from her. She is sure she has made the right decision. The warm weather down south is just what I need to make me well again. I can no longer stand these cold unforgiving northern winters. Last year's nearly finished me. It is still hard for her to accept the idea that her father is not the strong invincible man of steel she once knew. It makes her sad to see me in this new light. She swallows hard, clearing away the lump that has begun to well up in her throat.

The sound of the car engine roaring to life brings Julie's thoughts back to the present. Brian is already seated in the car ready to go. Sandra is trying, with limited success, to balance on the car's rear bumper. Julie takes a Kleenex from her coat pocket and wipes away any trace of evidence that might reveal what has just occupied her attention. Adequately composed, she gathers her lively little ball of delight and tucks her securely into the backseat of their "box on wheels" – the name that Brian jokingly uses to refer to their car. As she closes the door, she takes one last look back. Her eyes search the retreating horizon for some sign of her father. She can still just make out a speck way off in the distance among the brown fields, which are framed with streaks of grey leafless trees prepared for winter's coming reign. Finally, she sighs and says goodbye. Then, in a state of subdued hesitation, she climbs into her place of honor– the front passenger seat. Brian slips the gearshift with a certain grinding ease, and the little car pulls away bound for home.

CHAPTER 2

LEAVING ON A JET TRAIN

The taxi ride, the boarding of the train, and the train ride so far have all been uneventful motions. They have been interesting enough in their mildly amusing details. In my present state of mind though, they resemble little more than unsatisfactory fodder unable to come close to filling the void that now seems to occupy me. A feeling of numbness envelops me. I wonder if this is how it feels when your soul knows its journey through life is about to reach a conclusion— when it has grown so tired of living that it cannot help but take comfort in sleep. I feel tired right now.

The darkness flies past my compartment window with reckless abandon, content in the knowledge that it hides many secrets underside this blanket of night. Streaks of light pass me by unaware of my existence. I am unimportant to those who dwell behind the lights. Perhaps I hold no importance in anyone's life. Sure, I play a role in Julie and

Sandra's, but it has dissolved into a part played by a supporting actor at the most. I am nothing more than a mere extra, maybe a walk-on who has a few lines on occasion, in the play of Brian's life. Sadly, they are parts that if cut from the script, they can all do without and life will go on. How I long for the days past when I was central to my family's existence, I was relied on by the community, and I was an important cog in the wheel of the local economy. How did all that disappear and so fast? It didn't. It unraveled all too slowly over the years until now. Now I am little more than a burden upon the backs I once helped to strengthen. Old age has no place for pride. You soon come to realize that. You have no choice but to take what you can get and count your blessings.

These worried thoughts are making my eyes heavy; they are beginning to close under their own intuition. I look back at my solemn demise into uselessness- my steady decline towards the path I now tread. If only I had noticed the tell-tale signs occurring at the time- a lost step here, a forgotten name there. Perhaps somehow I could've corrected myself. It is the little things that are important. You don't become old in a day or even a year.

A little thing, which is somehow noticed and put right, can have a profound impact on the big picture. If enough of those little things are fixed quickly, perhaps you can halt time and even cheat death itself. It all comes down to being smart, keeping one step ahead of the game.

When I was forty-five, I began to notice a slight stiffness in my knees. It was nothing major, nothing to worry about. After all, I wasn't as young as I used to be, right? Wrong. That was my first mistake-accepting the inevitable and, therefore, doing nothing about it. If only I had realized the importance of the moment, I could have halted the crisis in its tracks. I should have started a vigorous exercise routine to bring elasticity back into my legs. Instead, I have allowed the condition to progress naturally to the point where I now have difficulty getting up out of a chair. You become old when you let yourself become old. If I had done something when I had the chance, I could still be a young man capable of just about anything. When I had to squint to see the numbers on the kitchen clock, what did I do? What else, I went and got glasses. Instead, I should've looked harder. When my hair started to reveal bits of grey, I should've cut the imposters out and forbid their return. A young capable man has no place for old man habits. A young capable man...

> *A young capable man is at the dinner table with his family. Margaret is seated at the far end close to the kitchen for convenient purposes. She has made her fish and chips; it must be Friday. I have to mow the lawn this weekend. I don't want to. I'd rather take a car trip or maybe go to the beach. Margaret still has that nice figure. I love looking at her in her new swimsuit. Julie is way down the beach building a sandcastle. There is no one to disturb us. We are all alone. I can hear the seagulls, and I can*

feel the closeness of the sea. The salty air is in my lungs; I can taste it. We are in the water. I am paddling to keep my head above the water. Margaret is swimming towards me, the bright sunlight glistening off her dark hair. She is so beautiful. I am so lucky. I love her so much. Our gazes are locked together. She has such beautiful eyes. Oh, how I love her. She is doing a striptease for me. She peels off her swimsuit. Her body has aged. Her breasts sag. Her skin is wrinkled, and her hair is grey and dull. I look away. When I turn back, she's gone. Through the water, I can make out a young woman swimming. The young woman is Margaret. I swim underneath the waves down towards her. As I get closer, she gets further away. I am running out of air. I can't breathe! I've got to get back up to the surface. I am trying to swim. My legs struggle to move. My knees are stiff. I can't breathe! I've got to keep going. This can't be real. I can't breathe! I've got to keep going! There's the surface. Just a little further. Gasp! I've broken through to the surface; I've made it!

The cool night air rushes into my lungs. I awake in a cold sweat gasping for air. None of it was real. Thank God! It was only a dream. It wasn't real. My heart races. I can still remember everything vividly: it is fresh in my mind. It all seemed so real that I thought I was going to die.

But it was only a dream. With this realization comes incredible relief, which helps me to relax. My breathing slows. My wife's young and old images leer at me still. In my dream, I was given the chance to connect with her again‑ as she was when she was still in her prime and it left my heart throbbing with overwhelming love. However, those burning passions were quickly doused in the wave of somber clarity that barraged me when I awoke. Even now, the sheer horror of seeing her old and withered body persists to terrify me and the crushing panic brought on by thinking I was going to die is slow in its retreat. Both will linger.

The remainder of the train journey is proving more enjoyable than I originally anticipated. I am impressed by the changing landscape, which seems to unfold for me like one of those flip the page books I used to read as a young child. The trees come alive with leaves where there once were none. The grass gets greener by degree, and I notice how the sun shines continuously during the day with an intensity that is all new to me. It has a soothing effect on me, almost to the point where I no longer feel the need to obsess about my worries. Maybe this isn't going to be so bad.

My destination is Bronsfield, a town just south of Atlanta, Georgia. There is supposed to be a rented condominium waiting for me upon my arrival. Brian and Julie made all the arrangements. Apparently, Brian has a brother-in-law who grew up in Bronsfield and he owns the apartment building. According to Brian, I am very lucky to get in on such short notice. It is lucky for me that some poor old lady died and created a vacancy. I think it would've been luckier for us both if she had lived. It wouldn't be on such short notice, either, if the two of them were not in so big a hurry to get me moving. I had every intention of staying right where I was. I had all the wood chopped, and the house was ready for the best winter could throw at us. Sure, they had been hinting since last spring that I should "consider the possibility of wintering down south at this point in your life" as they were so careful to phrase it. What did they mean "at this point in my life?" If I had no desire to live down south before why in the bloody hell would I want to go there now when I am too old to enjoy it? Maybe they are hoping it might help prolong my life. Well, maybe they are right there. The cold and dampness is beginning to get the better of me. I found that out last winter, but when they were pressing me for a decision on moving down there, it seemed that my life as it was wasn't much worth prolonging. I thought I should say my goodbyes while I still had a little shred of dignity left— go out while people still remembered me for who I used to be, not for what I had become. It was hard to know what to do. I had gotten to the point where I wasn't even sure what I wanted anymore, but I still wasn't completely convinced that retreating southerly for the winter was the absolute best thing to do. Come November, my mind was pretty well made up for me. Brian and Julie informed me they had heard of a condo being available. Believing that "such a golden opportunity" could not be passed on, Brian had already gone ahead and secured the lease. Despite my most blatant objections, I soon found that I didn't have a leg to stand on. When the alternatives, which they so cleverly attempted to disguise as being in my best interest, were attached to words such as "district nurse" and the much dreaded "old age home", I had little choice but to relinquish any fight left in me and wave the white flag of surrender.

Out of all the options, this journey south seemed my only means of retreat. Now they can feel secure in the knowledge they have assisted me in keeping some form of my independence with the added benefit of no longer having to watch me slowly die. If they aren't constantly reminded of the fact that I am dying, perhaps I won't die quite so quickly. Perhaps they won't want me to. I can't say I blame them in that respect. I now see this as my one last best chance. If I simply face the fact that my old life– the way it used to be– is over and behind me, it will be an absolute godsend to be able to go away and die with some independence and dignity just as an old dog sometimes chooses to go away and die. Out of respect for my family and with respect for myself I've chosen this path. They won't have to see those last few days of turmoil. They will remember me as a good father, a loving grandfather, a fair and agreeable father–in–law, a good and honest citizen, a vibrant individual, and a strong man. They will remember me the way I used to be and the way I always should be – if they haven't forgotten already.

CHAPTER 3

BRONSFIELD

Bronsfield seems like a nice enough town. It has an abundance of well-kept streets and houses, but it isn't too big. As the taxi passes through the final stretch of rural greenery and enters into the town limits, that familiar sign reads Population 6,300- not much more than back home. I expected more people to gather in a warmer climate. The cab driver is a black man who doesn't talk much and, not being an overly talkative sort of person myself, it has been a rather quiet ride. Bronsfield is about 30 miles, give or take, from Atlanta where my train journey ended. What little I saw of Atlanta seemed nice enough as far as cities tended to go, but as we passed through the grand old city, it was hard not to notice the urban decay taking place all around us. It is an unfortunate- although not uncommon- blight upon practically every American city of the day. There is nothing particularly new or surprising in the reasons for it. When you crowd too many people together, next thing you know everybody tries to get as far away from one another as they possibly can. Everybody wants their own space sooner or later. It is only human nature. Add to that the fact that industries and, therefore, jobs have been pulling out of the city cores on a vast scale over the past few decades. It leaves little for the inhabitants to do but not get along. It's surprising that there aren't far more gigantic ghost towns around.

I can't in all good faith say that I am a huge fan of cities. I was born and raised in a small town. And I have lived in one all my life and I am proud of it. There is a lot to be said about small town life. With the exception of growing up on a farm, a small town is the best place to raise a family. It is also a very pleasant place to come home to in the evening after work or to spend your weekend. My town has a strong sense of community. Everybody knows everybody, and you can trust in the knowledge that your children are safe. My God! It is still fairly safe to leave your doors unlocked and that really says something in this day and age. You can give me a small town like mine any day. It is even a great place to retire. Well, at least, it used to be. If there is one fault to be found with a close community, it is that too much genuine caring can work against you. I sometimes think that, at least in a city, no one really gives a fig when someone is holed up in their apartment waiting for the grim reaper to come a knocking. Those lucky bastards! Oh well, Bronsfield doesn't seem too bad at first look. I only agreed to come here because Brian and Julie's sales pitch made the place sound so inviting. It included the words "small town atmosphere" and "small town feeling", but the fact that it actually was a small town was what sold me on the idea.

The warm southern air flows in through the open car window. Everything is so green. The trees are rich in foliage, and the lawns look lush– even denser than the ones back home in early summer. I am surprised at how all this seems to have such an effect on me. It makes me feel as though spring has arrived after a long harsh winter. I remember the springs of my past: the grass turning green and starting to grow; the first flowers of the season beginning to show their bloom; leaves sprouting on the trees and birds singing; the rebirth of life taking place all around me as if in some form or sign of victory over the beast just slain; everything new again; nothing impossible; the world lying at my feet. It is strange how I feel that way right now. It is a nice feeling. I know I am still alive.

The taxi pulls up in front of a two storey building. It is kind of a little block of a building with rounded corners, and painted yellow to brighten its feel and give it a homier look.

"The Yellow Moon apartments. This is it. That'll be sixty-five dollars."

The cab driver utters his first words in just over half an hour. I almost expected him to take a few moments to figure out the amount, but it is clear that he is no stranger to the profession and knows his numbers. Mind you, the little time clock on the dash might've had a good bit to do with the promptness of his decision, although I don't think the clock is working correctly. During the ride, I observed that sometimes the numbers moved while at other times they did not. I can't help but wonder whether I am being overcharged. Maybe the decision did come a little too quickly as if it was just some number off the top of his head, but I'm not about to get into an argument with this husky looking fellow. Sixty-five dollars is quite a bit of money, but it isn't a case of me not being able to afford it. I have done well enough for myself over the years, so I am not uncomfortable in the financial department. However, I haven't gotten to this point by throwing good money away. Like a lot of things in my life these days, it looks as though I am just going to have to grin and bare it. The fact that he was carrying what looked to be a knife in his belt certainly played a role in the direction I took coming to that decision. I have also considered the idea that just because Harry Farlow back home takes three and a half minutes to figure out a cab fare for a ride a few miles long, it does not necessarily mean that the gentleman in question is not a little more sophisticated in his practice. So with the bags unloaded, the man is paid and the taxi speeds away leaving me to ponder my next move.

The lawn has been landscaped with the appropriate shrubbery and flower beds. The neatly sculpted trees are of southern varieties no doubt. Some of them resemble what look to be a form of cedar. There are also a few larger trees– a type of pine, I think. Regardless, lots worse things could pass for a view in any number of locations, so I feel fortunate enough with these circumstances.

Just as I am beginning to wonder how I should go about attempting to haul my five rather large suitcases up the walkway and in through the door, a young girl emerges from the building's entrance and offers assistance – not any time too soon either. Some of the people in the neighbouring houses were beginning to give me strange looks. Perhaps they wondered whether I was going to stand here all day in the midst of a pile of luggage not knowing my whereabouts and unsure of my next move. The girl who has come to my aid seems to be under a similar impression. She speaks to me in that soft reassuring fashion one would take if talking to a child or some unfortunate soul with Alzheimer's – neither of which would describe me. I can see though how it might be rather fortunate to be stricken with Alzheimer's. That way, at least half the time I wouldn't know what the hell was going on and the rest of the time I wouldn't know what I had missed and would be better off for it. The girl seems nice enough otherwise, so I guess I can forgive her ignorance. After all, maybe I do look a little confused.

She introduces herself as being Josie Spencer, the daughter of the man who owns the building. Her father is at a meeting this morning, so she has been left in charge to get me settled in. She picks up two of my bags and leads the way into the building. She informs me that she, her father, and Cloie all live together in one of the apartments on the second floor, and that I have the flat right below them.

"Which is lucky for you," she states, "so that you won't have to climb any stairs."

When she said that, I glared at her and that makes her laugh. She knows what I am thinking, and apologizes for her presumption that I am a complete invalid and, therefore, unable to manage even the most simple of tasks.

"I may be a bit short of wind and a little stiff in the joints, but I'm not ready for the wheelchair just yet,"

She looks at me with sort of a devilish twinkle in her eyes before relinquishing the words, "A little stiff is all it takes."

As that comment takes its time to register in my brain and I attempt to sort out its meaning, I can't help but be taken aback by the brashness of this young girl, who can't be more than sixteen. Before I can decide on how to respond to such a thing, she drops the suitcases inside the door to my flat and tells me to have a look around while she goes and gets the other bags. I turn to watch her glide down the hall and out the door, her long dark hair flowing behind her. She walks with such light steps that she almost floats. It is as if she bounces with every step she takes. She moves with such ease and carelessness that it truly astonishes me. I have forgotten how that feels. Ah, the magic of youth. It is just a faded memory to me, but I once knew that feeling of invincibility– the being that is youth. That is the key. If only you were able to get that back, you could live forever. And to think, I had it in the palm of my hand– this withered old hand I see before me now. Where did it go? How could I let it all go? Ah yes, youth is tricky– such a cunning beast. It does not leave you all at once. Its escape is slow; I hardly noticed its descent and now youth lays too far away for me to catch again.

"Don't look so confused, Pops. Have a look around the place, and make yourself at home. You're likely going to be here for a while; you might as well make the best of it. Just cuz your kids don't want you back home, it doesn't mean that we don't want you here. We're glad to have you– as long as you pay your rent, that is. Ha!" Josie laughs as she plops the last of my suitcases inside the door. She then flings herself on the couch in the center of my flat letting out a long sigh, "Well, I'm bushed."

My first thought is to scold her for not showing a little more respect towards her elders and to ask her to kindly leave. The way she conducts herself is rather a shock to me. I'm not used to that kind of behavior in my presence. I decide to bite my tongue, for in spite of all this and everything, the fact remains that she is still the first person who I have actually been able to carry on a conversation with since I left home. It would be foolish to pass on this opportunity so quickly. There is also the idea in my head that I like the way she comes right out and says what is on her mind. In fact, I think it to be a refreshing change. I am sick and tired of all the pussyfooting, sidestepping around issues, and other falsities that go on solely for the purpose of not hurting somebody else's feelings. I have been receiving far too much of that kind of treatment lately, and quite frankly, it has grown stale.

Feeling refreshed by my new found liberation, I answer, "Quite right. Right you are. Let's get me settled in. If this dump is going to be my home for the next six months, then I had best make the most of it."

I think I have gone too far with the 'dump' bit and half expect a good lecture on the exceptional qualities of this grand old building complete with references from the civil war; although, I am quite certain that its construction does not date that far back in time. Seventy-five years would be a better estimate. Instead, all I get is another taste of her sharp-tongued wit.

"Whatever you say old man, but you'll be doing the settling in bit all by your lonesome. I'm going out."

The old man comment hits me like a bullet in the back. It makes me realize how other people see me— not for who I really am but as this old withered hide I carry around on my extremities. The truth is that I have known it for a while, but sometimes I tend to forget, and these little reminders seem to hurt just as much as the first time I realized it. I have grown used to it by now, at least enough for the numbness to remain below the surface, so her thoughtless words will not succeed in completely ruining my new found good mood. I am more distraught with the notion I am about to lose my conversation sparring partner before I have a chance to really get into it. "Well, goodbye then, and thanks for the help, anyway. Josie, is it?"

"You know it is. And don't mention it: I was only too happy to help. My father should be back soon. He will help you with anything you need to get settled in. See yah." With that, she leaves. Once again I'm left alone to gather my thoughts and to take in the atmosphere around me.

My apartment consists of a large living room complete with furnishings: a sofa, chairs, coffee table. A bookshelf clings to the wall. A few out of date Reader's Digest magazines, a dictionary, and an old dusty Bible are its only contents. There is also a television set. I think I can even get cable- a convenience I never really felt the need for back home. I watch more T.V. now than I used to, granted, but I still prefer to read a good book. There is a small kitchen area attached to the living room- part of the same room, actually. Nothing too fancy, just a table with a couple of chairs. I guess they don't expect you to have your family over for dinner or even more than one guest at a time. I won't complain though. I am fortunate to get a place that has already been furnished.

The kitchen also includes an electric range and an older model lime green refrigerator. The old fridge seems to stick out like a sore thumb among the rest of the room's accessories. It just doesn't seem to go with anything, yet it still hums steadily along seemingly oblivious to the change occurring all around it. I can kind of relate to this fridge myself. It has served its purpose in life and outlasted the rest only to now find it is no longer appreciated for its efforts. Perhaps we have both come to this place to wait out our last few days together. I wonder which one of us will last the longer.

There is also a sink. I try both taps. The water seems to run alright. I open the cabinet underneath it. A bucket, a couple of sponges, and a rusty looking can of Drain-All are housed there within. The cabinets above the sink have even been stocked with a fair collection of mismatching dishes. I run myself a glass of water. I haven't had a drink since the train. What greets my mouth is cool, but the familiar taste of treatment agent spoils the occasion. I miss my home with its crystal clear, always fresh well water. What I wouldn't give to have a glass of it right now. This is another one of those instances where I don't know the good I have until it has been taken away from me. I should've brought a suitcase full of bottled water along with me. However, I didn't think of it at the time. Besides, I thought that five suitcases were plenty enough to be hauling around for such a distance. I couldn't very well take everything. It wasn't necessary, and it wasn't practical or, even more so, at all possible- not that I have any more material belongings than the average person, but the number of possessions a body accumulates over a lifetime is quite mind-boggling indeed. The house and garage back home are chalk full of life's little trophies, and those are just some of the things I have felt fit to keep. If I were to gather together all the things I have ever purchased, I would surely have enough stuff to fill a whole street of houses. It is kind of a waste when you look at it that way. Maybe not, a lot of those things brought me many more fond memories than they ever caused me grief. So seeing as memories are about all I am left with in life, I guess they were worth the trouble.

I have taken only a few of my most treasured belongings with me on this journey— things I cannot stand to do without: a small portrait of my wife in a hand-carved mother of pearl frame, which I have always kept on the bureau by my bed; the leather-bound Bible given to me at birth by my grandmother; and an old tattered family scrapbook containing the frozen photographic memory of every major achievement, date, moment, and chance meeting over the course of one family's life with a few locks of hair thrown in for good measure. Other than those, all I brought were basically clothes and other essentials. There was no sense in bringing along anything more. If I return to my home in the spring, there would be no need of it. And if I do not return, there would be no need of it either. When I die, Julie and Sandra can take what they want and the rest will be auctioned off into the hands of strangers from whence they came. Bahh! I hate to think from whence this water came. If I am forced to drink much of it, I am going to have to resort to buying bottled water. I used to think that was only the practice of trendy young people, but I am beginning to see the whole situation in an entirely new light. I can't say I

particularly blame them‒ not at all. A
voice startles me from behind.

"I see you're enjoying a glass of
Georgia's finest. It's nothing but the purest
swamp water in all the state. If you can
keep that down, you should handle our
cuisine just fine."

That is followed by a laugh, to which
I give my participation.

"Don't worry, you'll get used to it. It
will grow on you. And if it doesn't, you can
always do what I do‒ just drink bourbon.
Ha!"

By this time he has slid right up next
to me and is shaking my hand vigorously.

"How rude of me, let me formally
introduce myself. I'm Philip Peterson. I
own this place. You can call me Phil if you
like. Or some of my friends call me Pete.
That's fine too. Just don't call me P.P.
You know, peepee, as in the yellow variety.
Get it? Ha!"

I laugh again. I get it.

"Sorry that I wasn't here when you
arrived, but it couldn't be helped. I had a
meeting I just couldn't break. You know
how it is. But I trust that Josie got you
settled in alright?"

"Yes, she was very obliging. She
was quite helpful."

"Glad to hear it. She never lets me down. Sometimes I wonder who runs this place, her or me. It seems like she spends more time with the tenants than I do. I tell her she needs a hobby- something to get her out of the house more often. But you know how kids are. You can't understand them. They live in their own little world."

Can't that much be said of us all? But I know what he means. "I know how it is: I have a daughter and a granddaughter myself."

"God love 'em! Little women- the world can always do with more of those. You can't have too many or enough of them if you ask me. Yes sir."

This Phil seems to be quite the character. He seems to say exactly what is on his mind. I can see where his daughter gets it from. I wonder if all the men down here are that way. In small doses, it could be rather amusing, but if I have to put up with it day after day, it will soon grow tiresome. I am the sort of person who appreciates the quietness. When this guy is in the same room as you, it is like a three-ringed circus. It is almost too much for your head to contain. With each ring I go into, the act just gets larger and larger. I am beginning to get a little nauseous. I think he is going to go on and on, so I tell him he will have to excuse me, for I'm not feeling well after my long train trip. It is the truth about the not feeling well bit. The reason for my condition is less honest, but I can't very well explain to him that he is making me sick. He tells me he knows what I mean. Those train rides can take a lot out of a person; lots younger men than I have found themselves heaving off the end of a train station platform. If he doesn't leave soon, I am going to heave all over his new leather shoes. I hasten his departure by leading him towards the door. He can see I mean business, for my face is beginning to turn white— whiter than usual. So he tells me that if there is anything— anything at all— just to let him know and either he or Josie will fix me up straight away. He is sure I will soon feel right at home here: everybody in the building is just like family.

As we stand in the doorway to my apartment, he quickly explains that the paperwork has already been taken care of. Brian made all the arrangements. Wasn't that awfully nice of him? He even bought the train ticket— as if they don't think me capable of anything anymore. Maybe they thought I wouldn't leave if it was left up to me. Maybe I wouldn't have.

My only responsibility is to pay my rent on time. These kind folks down here are quite willing to take care of everything else I need assistance with. It seems that I don't have to do anything anymore. I wonder what they will do if I don't pay my rent. Maybe they will pay it for me. Then Brian and Julie will probably have me declared not fit and seize my bank accounts. Why not? They will have my money before long anyhow.

What is this? Phil is giving me a guided tour of the apartment before he goes- how thoughtful of him. Yes, there is the bathroom with a tub and a shower and two-tone floor tiles- very nice. And there is my bedroom- looks great. There is even a lovely view of the back garden from the window. What more does he say? There is a screen door so that I can step from the living room right out into the garden. This is too good to be true. My! Oh no, surely not. He doesn't say! Those are irises and at this time of year. And yes, I have already seen the rest of the place, but no, I haven't seen the rest of the building- just what I saw coming in. Yes, I will be sure to have him show me around the place tomorrow– once I have gotten settled in. No, I will not be a stranger because he certainly won't be. No, I don't imagine. Okay then, yes, I will be sure to have a good rest. Goodbye. I close the door behind him. My head is still spinning. The entire encounter was like an amusement ride gone bad. It is now over, and I am alone once again. My suitcases stare at me as they lay beside me in a pile just inside the door. They can wait until morning: they aren't going anywhere in particular. The thought of a soft warm bed appears mighty comforting to my weary soul. "Don't mind if I join you" says my back, and my tired legs follow close behind.

CHAPTER 4

SLEEPING BEAUTY

I awake the next morning feeling pleasantly refreshed. I haven't felt this way in quite a while. It has a lot to do with the atmosphere. The sunshine beams in through the bedroom window. Birds are singing right outside. A squirrel chatters away on the ground beneath a large old willow tree. It shelters the garden and protects it from the rays of the sun, not unlike a mother watching over her young. The early morning air is sweet and warm and fresh as Avalon in springtime in wedding dress.

Ahh! I breathe it all in. I have almost forgotten that which makes life worth living. These are all but things dreams surround. I am glad to be alive today. I once was lost but now am found. I take a deep breath and arise from my bed. I am still dressed in my clothes from the day before, now suitably wrinkled after their night's turmoil. I go to the window and gaze out into the garden taking in the wonderful scenery. My eyes bathe in the sights; my ears encompass the sounds, and my nostrils pull in the pleasing floral scents. There is something about early mornings.

To the right, my eyes catch a flash of pink. They are drawn over to the far side of the courtyard. There is a woman sunbathing on a lawn chair. She is lying on her stomach. I have to blink my eyes a couple of times just to make certain they are not playing tricks on me. She appears to be in the nude. I am rather taken aback by this sight. It seems they are a little freer in regards to such matters down here. Due to the warmer climate, perhaps they have grown accustomed to wearing fewer clothes, or maybe the woman simply doesn't expect any sightseers. I glance at my watch. It is only 6:30 a.m. and I figure that there aren't too many people— other than the squirrels— out and about at this time of morning to partake in the view. Maybe they sleep later down south. Regardless, she can't be too bashful. Just the thought of someone seeing me indecent would be enough to discourage the notion no matter how warm the sun felt on my bare skin.

I know I shouldn't, but I find myself unable to pull my eyes away from this motionless figure. I admire the fine curves of her hips. They are full and sumptuous. The sunlight glistens off her pink skin softening the illusion. Oddly, she doesn't appear out of place in this picture of cobblestones, flowerbeds, porcelain birdbaths, and cascading boughs of willow. She seems to subtly compliment the arrangement as if she were some Greek statue of water nymph origin.

A car horn sounds down the street reminding me that this scene must soon come to an end and scolding me for doing something I know well enough I should not be doing. It must have startled my sunbather as well for, before I can look away, she arises from the chair revealing a full frontal view. I didn't bargain on seeing such an eyeful: I didn't anticipate such a revelation. I am experiencing a strange mixture of guilt and pleasure. The bather, though womanly in all aspects of her beauty and physical attributes, is still but a girl. It is Josie's form my eyes follow. She walks back up the stairs and into her flat above mine seemingly unconcerned or unaware of her watcher. The pleasure I receive from this sight fills me with a warm feeling. The warm sensation growing inside me feels as though it is a rejuvenating force reawakening cells in my body I long thought dead.

My eyes lock onto a man standing in the window of the apartment across the square. He is staring right at me. He is watching, and he saw me watching the girl too. I am startled and stumble backwards falling onto the bed. My heart pounds. I look into the dresser mirror, and I see what he saw. The image returned by the glass is not one of comfort, but it is all too much the truth. What I see is an old pathetic pervert, so desperate to find some last spark of living in his fading life that he would resort to invading the privacy of an adolescent− a child− for the sake of his own pleasure. I feel embarrassed and ashamed for whom I have become. I am that strange old man I used to warn my daughter about. That revelation I cannot hide. I know it, and what is worse, the man across the square knows it too. Yet I am not alone in my guilt. I saw him watching too. He is just as guilty as I am. When he saw me, he didn't even seem startled. I think he was even smiling. What kind of a pervert is he? Maybe this sunbathing episode is a familiar routine for him. I feel a certain responsibility to alert Josie to this molestation of her innocence if only to lessen my feelings of guilt for my own participation in the unseemly event; however, by doing that, it will alert her to my involvement as well. What if she tells her father? He might throw me out of the building. What if word gets back to Brian and Julie? And Sandra— what will she think of her grandfather then? I won't be able to hold my head up in public; I am not that kind of person. It could ruin me. It will ruin me. But I hate the idea of this man continuing to watch her. It isn't right. Maybe, I should go and talk to him and reason with him. I doubt that he will say anything to anyone because, after all, he is as guilty as I am, maybe even more so. Maybe I can convince him to forget it ever happened. And if he stops watching her, we can put it all behind us as if it never happened. As for Josie, perhaps there is a more subtle way to advise her it is not such a good idea to continue this practice. I will get washed up and change my clothes. Then I will see what can be done to rectify this unfortunate situation. And to think the morning began with such promise. How quickly it has all deteriorated. Not more than fifteen minutes have gone past, yet so much has changed in a quarter of an hour.

I get washed up and put on a fresh change of clothes. In the process of dressing, I unpack some of my suitcases putting clothes in drawers and personal effects in the bathroom. It is now time to take my regular assortment of vitamins and doctor prescribed medications and to wash them down with a glass of the pungent swamp water that emerges with such a deliberate ease from my kitchen tap. This concoction is supposed to help keep me going, and today I feel I am going to need it more than ever. It does not look as though it is going to be an easy day. Maneuvering through it is going to require an awful lot of thought and will on my part. I would much rather go back to bed, bury my head and try to forget I even exist. But I have never been one for not facing up to my problems even if at times a bit reluctantly. I always come through and do the job when I have to. That is how I have always gotten through life and that is not about to change now, so it will be best to get to it.

I have come to the realization I am rather hungry. I haven't eaten since noon yesterday- the last meal they served on the train. My stomach is starting to growl. We can't have that! I have always firmly believed that the best way to start off your day is to have a hearty breakfast, but there is not a scrap of food in sight. The shelves are empty, and the only occupants of the old 'lime-o' – the name that I affectionately gave to my old war horse of a refrigerator – are a stale looking box of Cow Brand baking soda and a solitary egg in the egg rack.   I decide not to gamble on its freshness and attempt to whip up some form of egg and soda breakfast beverage. It isn't that I cannot cook for myself. Since Margaret passed away, I have managed to learn enough of the basics to adequately keep myself from starving, but given my earlier fortunes of the morning, I decide not to gamble on luck.   Instead, I will try out some of the local cuisine at a nearby restaurant and afterwards, I will pick up some groceries at the supermarket.   Until there is food in your fridge, you can't really call it a home, not even a temporary one.

On the way out, I check my pant pockets to make sure I haven't forgotten my wallet.   I have good reason for doing this.   On more than one occasion as of late, I did not take the time to check and I wound up paying for my negligence.   When you arrive at the cashier in a store and find you don't have any money to pay for the basket you have just tediously filled, it is an understatement to say it is slightly embarrassing, and I am not one to particularly enjoy a red face. It happens, but no matter how often it occurs, you never get used to it and it doesn't get any easier, even at my age. Nevertheless, I haven't forgotten my wallet this time around. Good. Then we are off.

A brief hallway with a door to either side leads to the front door, the one I came through the day before. From what I have gathered so far, the building is kind of a U shape with the courtyard being in the center of the U at the back of the building. There are at least five apartments on the bottom floor alone. Mine is located in the center at the front of the building. There is one on each side of mine and two more alongside the courtyard. The two rear apartments stretch the entire length of the courtyard with a stone wall completing the frame at the back of the garden. It is hard to say how many more are on the second floor. Maybe the Petersons, or is it the Spencers? No, Peterson. That's funny. When Josie was helping me with my bags, she said that her last name was Spencer. Yet she referred to Mr. Peterson as her father, I think. Yes, and his name is definitely Philip Peterson- unless she isn't his. No, he clearly made Josie out to be his daughter. Maybe she goes by her mother's maiden name. No, that wouldn't make any sense, either. Her mother would have to be Brian's sister to make Philip his brother-in-law, and Brian's last name is Leonard. I think Brian has two sisters. I have met Darlene several times but not the other one. Is she Josie's mother? Cloie? I thought her name was Francis. I am pretty sure it is. I don't know who this Cloie is but that was who Josie said lived in the apartment with them. I don't think Brian has ever mentioned anything about them splitting up or divorcing. But to tell you the truth, I don't recall him talking very much about Francis at all. I think he talks more about his brother-in-law Philip than he ever does about her, which is kind of odd. But I have always just figured that he and Francis aren't that close. Even when Brian told me that I would be living down here, Philip's name was the only one mentioned when discussing the arrangements. I guessed it was he who conducted the business side of things and that was why. But Brian never told me they weren't married anymore- unless he doesn't know. Even if he and Francis are no longer speaking to one another, you would think that Philip would say something about it on the phone- unless he is trying to hide something - I don't know what. Maybe I am just jumping to conclusions. Maybe it is something as simple as Francis going by her middle name. Maybe it is Cloie for all I know. I don't know why Josie does not refer to her as mom or mother; although, that isn't too unusual. That still doesn't explain why Josie said her last name was Spencer. It is possible she was adopted and has kept her original name. Brian has never said whether they have kids or not, so I don't really know. Maybe that is it. And of course, there is the possibility she was only fooling when she told me her last name was Spencer. All I have to do is ask. It is strange how I think of all this now and none of it sunk in when they were telling me these things yesterday. It is not surprising, though. While Philip was droning on about everything, I was barely conscious. I was pretty tired. I imagine it just needed time to register.

I walk out into the fresh morning blue. The clear, unmovable sky surrounds the entire town. It gives me a welcome sense of security as I tread on into strange new territory. The building I am staying in is situated not far from the center of town. Within a block and a half, I am walking past stores and shops. After passing by a Chinese place and a fried chicken joint, I go into a little café, which appears clean and pleasant. A round little man of black origins stands behind the counter. He has on a white apron and is reading a newspaper. An older man and his wife are having breakfast at one of the half dozen tables set around the small room. I order the breakfast special, which consists of two strips of bacon, a couple of runny fried eggs, some toast, a bran muffin, a glass of orange juice, and a cup of coffee. I don't think it matters where a person goes in America: every restaurant seems to serve the exact same breakfast and the eggs are always runny. You would think they could at least take the meager amount of time it requires to cook them right, especially down in this part of the country. I could get salmonella. That would be fun. I could spend my last few days on this earth perched on the toilet. That might be rather fitting. I sit down at a table by myself and eat the first breakfast of the rest of my life. If this is any indicator of how the rest of my life is going to be, I will be having a bowl of cherries for breakfast next time. Even though I hate wasting food, I can down only the one egg. The other I will leave as a tip. I am disappointed. I hoped for a more savory outcome. However, I will be back to eat another meal here, for it is not at all lacking in atmosphere or character, which are important qualities when choosing a particular place to break bread. The proprietor is sufficiently friendly and non-threatening in appearance, which always helps to encourage one's appetite. Also, I am not about to base my entire judgment on what is really only a small portion of a single meal. Until I have tasted the lunch and dinner specials, I am in no position to put forth any criticisms— over and above the comment on the runny eggs. So, all willing, I will be back. That is not to say I will not choose to frequent other dining establishments around the local area. After all, I will only have to be fair.

After making enquiries in the café as to the whereabouts of the closest grocery store, I continue with my exploration of this strange new land. As I strike forth down the paths of concrete and stone, I admire the architecture of the downtown buildings noticing how everything seems to fit together so well. The idea occurs to me that the South really knows how to make you feel at home. There is just the right mixture of grand old mansions, little white churches, and freshly painted clad board houses- all blended together with streaks of green lawn and hanging willow trees and held secure under the blue American sky. The cities hold no illusions when compared to towns like this. These are the hometowns of America where boys grow up to become men and where girls become young ladies. These towns are where governors emerge from and where Presidents go to die. My town is a town such as this; however, the South is different. There is something about the South; there is a reason why the crow flies south for the winter.

CHAPTER 5

ENCOUNTER AT LEIGHBRANT'S

I find myself standing outside the Leighbrant grocery. This looks to be just the place to provide me with what I am in search of. I go inside and park myself behind a cage on wheels. That is my preferred term. Some choose to call them grocery shopping carts. The first thing I do is pick up a local newspaper. If I want to know what is going on in this town, that is the place to begin. Leighbrant's is a fair sized store- not like one of those large commercial chain stores, but it is certainly quite large enough to serve half the town. From what I understand, along with Leighbrant's, there is another supermarket on the other side of town. This one is a little more convenient, for it is within walking distance of my apartment, so I have no intention of comparing prices. I put a couple of loaves of bread in the cart, some cheese buns, donuts- I like the honey-dip kind- and that's it for the bakery section. I shove my cart around the corner and into the next aisle only to come face to face with the man from the building who was watching me and Josie earlier this morning. He is pushing a grocery cart. He too has gone out in search of sustenance. The colour drains from my face. I don't know what to say. I planned on talking to him about the incident later today. I hadn't quite decided on how to go about it yet, so I am not prepared for it now. I'm not certain if he even recognizes me at first. But then a smile comes over his face— that same smile I saw from his window— and I know he knows. Before I can make up my mind whether to say anything or not, he breaks the silence.

"Well, hello there, stranger, imagine meeting you here. I guess I'm not the only early bird in town."

"No, I guess not," I reply rather sheepishly, still unsure.

"Don't be shy now. I know you. You're from my building. You just moved in yesterday. I saw you..."

Maybe he didn't recognize me in the window. Perhaps he only saw me yesterday when I arrived. Maybe I have dodged a bullet this time. Just as I am beginning to feel a pang of relief, he continues.

"I saw you this morning."

My heart sinks, and he continues.

"I saw you across the square. You were gazing from your window. Lovely view, isn't it?"

My mouth drops open, but I can't find any words. If there was any colour left in my face after the initial shock of seeing him here, it now drains away completely. I start to stammer. "I– I– I don't know what you are talking about."

"Oh", he quickly cuts in, "but I think you do. You know precisely what I am talking about. Don't get me wrong. I'm not saying I blame you. What kind of a red-blooded Southern man wouldn't sneak a peek, especially when it is in his own backyard? The way I see it, if she didn't want to show it off, she wouldn't be so open in her display. Would she? To tell you the truth, I wouldn't be surprised at all if she likes it– if she takes some weird sort of erotic pleasure in watching us squirm. Come on! Why else would she be laying out there in the flesh like that?"

A respectable looking lady passes us by with her cart and gives me a dirty look. I blush and look away down towards the cans of peas pretending that I too am just an innocent bystander and not part of this conversation, which she might or might not have just overheard. I guess she has heard enough of it and hence the dirty look. I don't take this lightly. It wasn't so long ago as yesterday I still considered myself to be a respectable member of society, but now, today, it is apparent I have fallen several levels. I am presently on par with the man here beside me, who is obviously of questionable moral character. If this is one of my newly acquired peers, I'm not very pleased with my new standing within the social scheme of things. However, that is certainly a relief in a way— that he takes this unseemly sort of behaviour all so lightly. To him it obviously isn't any big deal. To me, on the other hand, it still is. But if he is offering me forgiveness for my actions, I am not so foolish as to decline. I can see it would be futile to try and convince him that his part in all this is in the slightest bit wrong — that his actions are stripping away what little is left of the poor girl's innocence. That notion is beginning to sound a little ridiculous, even to me. If I am having difficulty trying to convince myself of her innocence, I would certainly have a time convincing a red-blooded Southern man of his wrongful ways. It would be so much easier to simply try and fake a smile. So that is exactly what I do when I answer him by saying, "I guess you have a point there."

"Not here, but I did have one there this morning. And I bet that you had one too. Eh, isn't that right, you old rascal?"

With that, the same lady who passed us in the aisle a few minutes earlier gives me another dirty look. She then wastes no time at all in hightailing it around the end of the row. I am beginning to wonder whether all Southern men behave in this way, or perhaps I just tend to draw to me the exceptions. Philip Peterson and this fellow would get along just smashing, I think. They are both larger than life characters whose sense of humour seems to scrape the bottom of the barrel when it comes to being in good taste. However, I hope that Philip's character holds a little more in the way of decency because, after all, he is practically family— practically. Having grown exhausted with the conversation by this point and wanting to get out of here before drawing anymore attention to myself, I put forth the excuse I want to finish up my shopping and get back home before things get too crowded closer to midday. Truthfully, there is no real hurry to get home. It isn't as though I have a full list of scheduled events for the rest of the day or anything. In reality, I will probably just go home and take a nap, but it is the best thing I can come up with at this time that sounds as plausible as possible. Just when I believe my cleverness has prevailed, he halts my retreat yet again.

"Before you go running off with your tail between your legs- since we are going to be neighbors- we had best formally introduce ourselves."

I had hoped to avoid that pleasure. He holds out his hand.

"I'm Rex Targent."

I pause momentarily then finally give in. I clasp his outstretched hand and return the pleasantries. As our palms mesh together in this time honoured ritual of comradeship, I know I am throwing in with the devil, and that my life can only turn for the worse because of it. As my palm soaks up his oils, I become sickened by that notion. In life you tend to meet friends in all sorts of strange ways. I never thought myself the kind of man who would associate with someone like this guy Rex, but it seems that these days I am doing a lot of things I never thought I would be doing before. In truth, I'm not even close to being the man I used to be. As the oil works its way deeper into my skin, Rex's character— or perhaps, his lack of it— seems almost appealing. I release his grip and make my departure before I consider these thoughts too seriously. Before I can fully complete my escape though, he puts forth an invitation for dinner and drinks at his place this evening so that we can become better acquainted. That thought more than just a little bit scares me, seeing as it is the first invitation of sorts I have received since my arrival or, for that matter, in quite a while. At home everyone seems set on trying to get rid of me, yet here is someone who actually appears to want to get to know me, so he can't be all that bad. Maybe this seedy man is a more decent and caring human being than all those supposedly good outstanding people who have surrounded me my entire life. Certainly, at the very least, he is worthy of being given a chance to prove himself one way or the other. So seeing as I don't really know anybody else down here well enough to have them invite me out for dinner, along with the fact that I am still under the impression I am in a big hurry to get out of here and am not thinking at all clearly, I accept.

After finishing up my grocery shopping and successfully avoiding Rex for the rest of my time in Leighbrant's, I now ready myself for the return home. I pay at the cash and start to roll my cart load towards the door only to find that a new problem presents itself: I have bought far too many groceries for me to carry home myself. Now what am I going to do? I can't possibly carry this much home with me. With everything preoccupying my mind, I haven't been thinking. I just assumed I had a car. In the past 50 years, I have never been without one- at least, not until I moved down here. This is going to take some getting used to. I didn't think that I would need one down here. The ironic thing is that while Rex was driving away in his car, I was busy hiding behind boxes. Otherwise, I could've likely gotten a ride home with him. Seeing as I will be having dinner with the man in his home tonight, it might have been fitting. The clerk at the checkout must sense my dilemma, for he enquires whether I will be requiring the grocery's home delivery service. That can easily be arranged if I don't mind waiting until afternoon for my groceries. I gladly accept. I ate a large enough breakfast to tide me over until then. After all, at my age, I find I do not eat as much as I used to. When I attempt to disregard the fact that my stomach is gradually shrinking and choose to ignore the warnings, the rest of my bodily functions soon expose my error in judgment and, in doing so, can make my life extremely uncomfortable. So therefore, I have come to accept and to even respect this newfound truth in my life– I have to. I thank the store clerk and tell him that I will carry one bag home myself. I take the one with the donuts just in case I happen to get hungry and feel in need of a little something between now and delivery time. He smiles kindly as I leave the store. Perhaps it is because I am old and he feels some sort of understanding towards life and old age itself, or maybe he just thinks me to be a rather pleasant person. Pleasantness always helps to make everyone's day a little brighter. I am glad I can be pleasant.

CHAPTER 6

POOR OLD MRS. GRIMSON

I arrive back at my building after a leisurely walk home. I am pleased to say my knee joints aren't giving me too much trouble. Maybe it has something to do with the warm weather. If I were back home and walked that far, especially at this time of year– in November– my joints would stiffen up. Now even my wind is pretty good. As long as I don't try to walk too quickly and overexert myself, I will be just fine. My lungs feel clearer than they have felt in quite a while. As I walk up the walkway to the apartment house, I am met by Philip.

"You're just the man I've been wanting to see."

"Oh," I said. I am a little apprehensive about why he wants to see me.

"Yes sir, I've been knocking on your door for the past hour– off and on. I was beginning to wonder whether something had happened to you. God forbid! But you can never be too careful when people get to be your age, you know. That's how it was with poor old Mrs. Grimson. We hadn't seen or heard from her in days; although, that wasn't particularly out of the ordinary for her. She would often remain in her apartment for days on end without emerging. I generally try to check on all the tenants at least once every couple of days, but depending on how busy I am with other things, I don't always get around to it. You know how it is."

"Yes," I say.

"And it was one of those weeks where I didn't know whether I was coming or going. I think I knocked on her door one day and there was no answer, but I just figured she was in the tub or taking a nap or something. I didn't want to disturb her, so I didn't bang too long. Anyhow, I can't say for sure whether it had happened by that time or not. It's hard to say. You see, the guy from the hospital− the coroner or whatever− said she didn't die right away. It could have been days before she actually passed, which makes me feel kind of guilty− her lying in there all that time like that while we were just a few yards away. If only she had called out or something, but I guess she was too weak. Besides, the doctor said she probably couldn't have spoken anyway. The stroke she had suffered had paralyzed all one side of her body. That didn't kill her though. Apparently, she got so weak from lack of food and water that she literally starved to death until her heart finally gave out. The poor old thing. Like I told the police, I felt awful, but what was I supposed to do about it? I had no way of knowing. I'm just surprised that Josie didn't notice anything wrong. My own daughter spends more time with the people who live here than I do. When I can't find her, she's usually in one of the apartments or out back in the garden chattin' it up with somebody. She's pretty familiar with just about everyone around here. She often used to spend time talking to Mrs. Grimson, but I guess that she had no way of knowing, either. Actually, it was Josie who finally alerted me to there being something not quite right. One day she was out in the garden and she thought she smelled something funny- like a dead rat or something. So she went and got me, and I could smell it too. At first I thought that maybe the old refrigerator in there had finally given out and some meat had gone bad or something. You know, down here in the South with all the heat it doesn't take long for that to happen. I did know Mrs. Grimson had a cat which she used to buy hamburger for. Even though I have a no pets policy here in the building, I made an exception for her because she loved that old cat so much. She'd had it since it was a kitten, and after her children had forced her out of her home, her cat was the only thing she really had left. Her kids never came to visit her or anything, so I kind of felt sorry for her. After all, it was only one old cat – but never mind all that."

"I knew the old girl's smell– sense of smell– wasn't any too good, but I also knew it was time to check into it. I don't like intruding on people's privacy and letting myself into tenant's rooms because most people don't take too kindly to that practice– not that I blame them. I let them have their space and I have mine. As long as they pay their rent on time and behave themselves, that's all I ask. Seeing as most of my tenants tend to be seniors, I generally don't have any trouble in either of those respects. This time, though, I knew I had better make an exception because, after all, there comes a time when the tenant's well being has got to be considered. So when I opened the door, I wasn't really prepared for what awaited me in there. It was not rotten hamburger we smelled. She was lying there on the floor not more than six feet from the back patio doors. If the drapes had not been drawn closed, someone would have noticed her lying there long ago. I think she had been dead for at least a couple of days, and by the look of things – Lord knows how long she had been lying there. It could have been for days. Her eyes were still open– not glossy but kind of dull. You know, blank looking. They were sunk straight into her head just staring. They were fixed on the ceiling with her mouth wide open like it was frozen there. She was lying on her back, and her dress was all stuck to her body with dried excrement. It was just a vulgar smell. Josie was with me, and she had to run outside and bring up. I almost did myself."

"If that wasn't bad enough, the cat was lying there beside her – dead too. My guess is that old age had finally caught up with the cat, and when she found it, the shock was simply too much for her to take. Believe me; you don't want to stumble upon something like that. I still can't get the image out of my head, but I guess it was fitting they should both go together. So anyway, you can see why I'm now a little overcautious with the welfare of my tenants. I don't want something horrible like that to happen again, especially in your apartment. The police might begin to wonder what is going on in there."

I stood there dumbfounded as the story only got worse and worse almost in disbelief of what my ears were hearing. Now I'm not going to be able to get the image out of my head, either. Every time I look at the spot where she fell, I am going to see those rotting corpses and envision her and her cat lying there. Sometimes you would rather not know certain things, and this is one of those times.

Not that this sort of thing particularly scares me, I just don't like the idea of something of this nature happening in the place where I am living. It kind of sends a chill down my spine. Like most people, I don't know whether I believe in ghosts or not. I'm not one to fool myself into denying their outright existence, but at the same time, I have never really witnessed any evidence to lend support to the contrary. From my limited knowledge of the internal workings of the world, I consider it reasonable to assume they might exist. To be entirely truthful, I have never really given the idea too much serious thought.

I have never been what you would call an overly religious person. I did what I believed was my duty and went to church-on a semi-regular basis- and I made certain that my family was brought up the right way with the church being an important part of their lives. Being a Protestant, maybe the spiritual side of things isn't quite as deeply rooted in me as it is in some people. I know my wife, Margaret, was a more spiritual person than I can ever hope of being. I don't know how to explain it other than by saying that it was right for her, it was who she was. With that sort of thing, that is the way it has to be. You can't really explain it. You just have to know yourself- know it in yourself. Maybe it was because of her Roman Catholic upbringing. Maybe that had something to do with it. I don't know. I find that Catholics are either more open to believe in the spiritual world or just the opposite. For some, nothing exists outside of dying and going to heaven or hell- one or the other. There is no room in their beliefs for anything in between or outside that permanent exact structure.

Under the circumstances, maybe it is just as well that I don't believe too deeply, for as I am growing older and closer to the inevitable- closer to my time- I tend to find myself opening up to possibilities that I would've never seriously considered before. For the first time in my life, I don't really know where I am going. All my life up until now I pretty well knew exactly what I was going to do: play ball in high school.

Even after being drafted into the war against Germany, all I thought about was returning home and marrying my sweetheart. Though the horrors of death were all around me for almost three years, I never really considered dying to be a viable option. Margaret was waiting anxiously for me back home, and who was I to disappoint her. Something as trivial as a World War wasn't going to prevent my life from continuing its rightful course. Maybe that unwavering determination was what brought me through it intact- something did.

When I arrived home after the war, Margaret and a good job were waiting for me. We bought a house and made a home. We had Julie and brought her up right. The years passed by, and everything fell into place just as it had been written- just as it was meant to be. I never questioned anything. Even when Margaret died, I accepted it. I have come to accept it. Now I find myself questioning everything. I have no idea where I am going. I am even uncertain about today.

The thing that scares me the most isn't the threat of that old lady, who died in such a horrible way, coming back and haunting my apartment. It has more to do with the fact that that could be me in the not too distant future lying there alone in death's clutches, helpless, lingering in life's last stages fearful of the great abyss- the unknown. The notion that I can so closely relate to that lonely old woman scares me most of all- the fear of fear's uncertain certainty.

This grey feeling overwhelms me making me tired. I tell Philip I am going to go in and take a nap, ghost or no ghost. He tries to the best of his ability to assure me that there is no ghost in my apartment that need worry me: old Mrs. Grimson is resting in a much kinder and gentler place now. The only trouble is that I don't think he actually believes it himself. He has a frightened look about him. Maybe he has seen something. I wonder why he is telling me all this. It would be enough to drive most people away. I now understand why I was able to get this place on such short notice– lucky ol' me. It is as if something is weighing heavy on his mind. It is worrying him, like he feels obligated to tell me this out of some sort of a sense of guilt. It makes me think he has seen something. I stare hard at him to see if I can force him into revealing something further. Alas, there isn't anything more forthcoming; although, he does look rather surprised at how well I have taken it all and appears more than just a little relieved he has gotten it off his chest. Maybe he figured it was better to tell me himself before I heard word of it from somebody else. I imagine that Rex Targent will be only too glad to leak the grizzly details before long. Perhaps he even has plans for such things over dinner tonight. So figuring that is all the informative conversation I am going to extract from Philip's person on this occasion, I start to go through the doorway only to be halted by Philip's somewhat frantic outburst.

"Wait, wait! What I wanted to talk to you about. With all that talk about Mrs. Grimson, I almost forgot why I was trying to get hold of you. Your daughter telephoned earlier this morning when you were out. She wanted to make sure you had arrived safe and sound."

"Oh shoot, I should have called her last night to let her know I had gotten here alright. It completely slipped my mind. After you left yesterday, I just went straight to bed. I was so tired. Then this morning I didn't even think of it." I am upset with myself for my lack of responsibility. Julie will be worried sick.

"Ah, don't worry about it. I told her you had gotten settled in just fine. I said you were a little groggy after your trip but still in one piece, which was pretty good for an old timer, I thought. She wanted to speak to you, so I ran down and knocked on your door, but when there was no answer, I told her you were still sleeping, and that I would have you call her when you woke up. She said not to bother, though. She just wanted to make sure you had arrived safely. She understood you had probably just forgotten to call. She said to give you her love and so did Sandra and Brian. Sandra must be your granddaughter. She must miss her grandpa."

I feel so useless. I am so old that I can't even remember something as important– or as simple– as preventing those who are dear to me from worrying themselves to death that something has happened to me. I can't remember anything anymore and it seems Julie expects that of me. It doesn't surprise her any when I fail to call. She knows I am old and useless. That was why she sent me down here. I'm not fooling anyone. I'm not even fooling myself anymore. I can't be depended upon for anything and that is the hardest part for me to accept. At least Sandra, my sweet little Sandra, won't have to see what her grandfather has become.

"Are you sure she didn't want me to call her back?"

"Oh no, I told her that I'd take good care of you. She said that she'd call back sometime next week to see how you were getting along. I told her that maybe we'd have a phone put in your apartment by that time, and then she could call you directly."

I am beginning to wonder whether what he is saying is true; maybe I do need somebody to look after me. Maybe I am no longer capable of taking care of myself. I hate to admit it, and I'm not even sure that I believe it. I do know one thing: I am pretty certain that Philip Peterson is not the man for the job, particularly in view of the swell job he did looking after poor old Mrs. Grimson.

I wonder why there isn't a phone in my apartment already. I ask Philip about that, and he informs me it is his policy not to install a phone unless the tenant requests it. I think that rather odd, but he insists it just makes sense. He explains that half his tenants actually prefer not to have a telephone.

"Most don't have many relatives who actually take the time to call them, and they don't want to be bothered by crank callers or surveys. If they need to make or receive any important calls, they are free to use the phone up in my flat, or I can make the calls for them. It's the same thing with driving a car. The only tenant who has one is Mr. Targent. All the rest, I am only too happy to drive them wherever they want to go. We are like one big happy family here; we look out for one another. So if you should have any errands needing doing, or if you need to go downtown for anything, all you need to do is ask me or Josie and we'll take care of it for you. If I had known you needed to do some grocery shopping, I would have driven you. Next time be sure to let me know. Some of the tenants even give us a list, and Josie gets their groceries for them. We can do it either way, whichever you prefer."

I think that to be very considerate of him, so I tell him that next time I will accept his hospitality and take him up on his offer to drive me. It will certainly come in useful because I do not intend to buy a car. Walking is okay when I don't have to carry anything or go too far, but when I do, a free ride will really come in handy. Besides, it will be a big savings not having to tip the grocery delivery guy every week.

Philip and I part company, and I return to my flat. Now feeling the effects from my day's activities, I decide to self-medicate with a donut and a glass of grape juice. I possessed the good sense to purchase the grape juice so that I wouldn't have to tolerate another glass of my building's horribly poor excuse for drinking water.

After contenting my stomach and appeasing my thirst, I stretch out on the couch. The room temperature is just right for sleeping. The shade of the indoors is refreshingly cool, and a soft breeze blows lightly in through the screened patio entrance fluttering my shirt sleeves and tenderly caressing my skin. The sunshine's warmth cascades in through the screen falling delicately as little diamond shaped specks on my chest. I soak up the warmth and savor the cooling refreshment as they melt together as one. I let my body go limp and soon am fast asleep.

A hollow knocking sound in the distance wakes me out of my restful state. My arm dangles over the end of the couch and falls toward the floor. Without warning, it touches the carpet. I jump up with a start! The hair on the back of my neck stands up, and my body is alert with a cold sensation. A strange feeling runs through me sending a chill down my spine. The image of the old lady lying there on the floor beside the sofa is fresh in my mind. I stare at the floor. I am now fully awake. The persistent knocking takes hold of my attention. I push the terrible image away and go on and answer the door.

My groceries are here. I thank and pay the delivery man, sending him on his way with all the usual pleasantries afforded to such strangers. With that task complete, I start to put my groceries away, but I am having trouble trying to focus. The image is still there. When I look at the spot where she fell on the floor, I can see her clear as day. When I close my eyes, there she is. I try to concentrate on putting the food into its proper place, but I can't block it out. This experience frightens me and I didn't expect that. After talking to Philip, I didn't even give it a second thought. I got back to the apartment, and I simply lay down and went to sleep. I don't remember dreaming about anything. I just heard the knocking in the distance. Then my fingers touched the carpet and this feeling rushed over me – all of a sudden – as if it had come out of nowhere. I don't like this feeling at all. I don't get scared easily, but from what little experience I do have, I know that this is how it feels.

Memories come back to me of being a boy and lying awake at night in the midst of the pitch blackness after being awakened out of a dream. I see the hushed room and feel the cold sweat soaked sheets clinging to my skin. My heart races with a feeling of intense fear. The darkness of night is all around me, and it makes me freeze in terror. I used to cover my head with the blankets and pray that it would all go away – and how it all did – eventually. That is how I feel right now, yet I know it isn't a dream, and I am now too old to cover my head with the blankets and hide from my fears. Still, I hope it will gradually fade away this time as well. I don't know why I feel this way or what exactly the cause of it is. Perhaps in old age you become as you are in youth- more sensitive to the presence of things unseen. I need to get a grip on myself. Maybe I could go out for another walk.

I pick a street and begin to walk down it. Block after block steadily recedes behind me until I come to a park. A creek flows through its center with a little oval bridge crossing it. I find a bench beside the water and watch the swans and geese for a while. Watching them float around on the green, shaded surface off side of the sunlight is very peaceful. There is hardly an intruder to interrupt my peace. A couple of school kids walk through the park, no doubt on their way to some routine adventure. A middle-aged woman with dyed hair and too much makeup for mid-afternoon comes along walking a little dog. Undisturbed by that, I take rest. Before long, I am drifting into a deep, peaceful sleep. When I awake a couple of hours later, I feel renewed once again.

CHAPTER 7

AN EVENING WITH MR. TARGENT

Now, what is next on my agenda? Ah yes, I am to have an evening in‑ or should I say out‑ with that seedy neighbour of mine, Mr. Rex Targent. Wait now, that is not exactly fair. I will at least have to get to know the man a little better before I go passing judgment. However, from what I have seen of him so far, my first opinion might not be that far off. Oh well, he is the only friend I have. Ooh, that sends a shiver down my spine and makes me cringe at the very thought: my best friend just happens to be a somewhat seedy pervert. Things are going well for me, aren't they? If I were doing any better, I'd be dead. I am a real winner.

Back home I never really felt the need to have any what you would call close friends. The only one whom I really needed for friendship was my wife, Margaret. She was friend, lover, mother, nurse, a shoulder to cry on‑ everything to me. Since she died, I have been without a friend and I will never have a friend like that again. When you depend on one person for all that– for all those things– for such a long time, nobody else can really take their place and you just have to accept that. Maybe once you've had someone in your life like that, you never really need another and maybe you are not granted another.

Throughout my life, there have been certain neighbors and coworkers whom I could have called friends. Some of those people have probably considered me their friend while I have looked upon them more as being folks who are simply nearby whom I get along well with. I suppose that if they are not your enemies, you could refer to them as friends. Maybe they have been my friends, but still, that is a pretty broad term.

Before Margaret died, she and I lived beside the same neighbors for over forty years, and even though they were friendly enough and we got on very well, I can't remember having a meal in our home with any of them. That pleasure was solely reserved for family and in-laws – oh yes, and of course, the minister. About once every year he would make a point of coming around for a meal on a summer's evening where we were obliged to exchange pleasant conversation for an hour or so, whether we felt like it or not. If I can remember correctly, it always rained when he was over for dinner. It was always on a rainy evening for some reason or another. I think we had him at noon once, and it rained that time as well. Even then, we never had a heart to heart with him.

Some people seem able to open up to just about anyone. The whole world tends to be their friend. Margaret and I were never like that‒ I wasn't, anyhow. I don't know about Margaret. She might've had one or two fairly close lady friends whom she had known since childhood, but I don't think she told them everything. She was dignified like that. She had her pride, and there were certain things she did not discuss. There are certain things between a man and his wife that are just between the two of you. Margaret and I shared many secrets over the course of our marriage. Of all the things I have lost in my life, those I've kept safe. I will take them to the grave with me, but I wouldn't mind having a friend of sorts right now, someone just for a little company to keep me from being completely alone. I find myself more in need of such companionship now than ever before.

How things change. After Margaret died, I still had Julie and then Sandra. Brian is okay, but I would certainly never call him a friend. I don't know if I can call my child my friend- or the same of my grandchild. Yet if I cannot refer to them as friends, then what can I call them? If they cannot be my closest to the heart, perhaps I am meant to be alone. They are my blood- the fulfillment of my love. They are an extension of me. They are not only part of me, they are who I am. I should love them as I love myself. Maybe... I will wear a tie.

Rex said to be over at his place for dinner by around 6 o'clock. As I stand outside my doorway, I glance at my watch. It is 6:03 in the p.m. Beyond the Yellow Moon apartments, the sun sinks beneath the horizon signaling an end to another day- the occasion being marked by twilight. I stop and admire the natural beauty for a moment before walking around by the street to the front door of his flat. I do this rather than cutting across the back garden and entering by the patio door. I figure we are not quite that informal as of yet for us to be climbing in each other's rear windows.

Rex's apartment doorway is located on the outer south side of the building. It and the one on the north side are the only ones on the bottom floor that can be reached from directly off the street. Mine and the two out front have to be reached by going in through the front door and entering by the hallway. My apartment, Rex's, and the one along the north side are also equipped with back patio doors which open onto the garden square. After ringing the doorbell, as I stand outside the door awaiting Rex to answer, I notice a light come on in the room up above me. In the light that falls to the ground from the window, I can see shadows moving about very quickly. It reminds me of a projector casting down images on a screen. I can also make out voices. They are raised to a heightened level as if they are arguing. I can't tell what they are saying, but it sounds like a man and a woman, and the man sounds like Philip Peterson. Just now, Rex comes to the door.

"Why, hello there, stranger, you're right on time."

He can see I have been listening to the dramatic episode up above.

"Ah, don't mind that. I hear it too. They go at it like cats and dogs sometimes.

When it gets too loud, I just turn the music on."

He has the music on now.

"Does he argue like that with Josie?" I wonder aloud, for I am unsure whether it is Josie's voice I hear or not.

"Oh no, not usually, anyhow, that's Cloie. I'm surprised she hasn't packed up and left him long ago. They always seem to be at each other's throats. They can't seem to agree on anything."

"What do they argue about?" My interest has been peaked by the mention of this, so far, mysterious lady. I have yet to see her. The only mention of her came from Josie when I checked in. I had begun to wonder whether or not she even existed. Even though I have been here only a little over a day, I still think it rather strange.

"They argue about anything and everything under the sun: from her being too extravagant, to him not being extravagant enough, from her wanting to eat grass and rice, to him wanting to eat a buffalo. Maybe he left the toilet seat up again. I don't know. It could be anything this time. I'm not psychic, so your guess is as good as mine. Maybe they're arguing over Josie. They have been known to do that on a few occasions."

Seeing a golden opportunity to answer the nagging question that has been wearing on my mind, I jump at the chance. "Is Cloie Josie's mother?"

"God no," Rex retorts back, almost to the point of yelling.

He seems shocked I would even think it.

"Cloie is just his latest pleasure puff. She gives him what he needs, and he spends money on her. It's quite a practical arrangement really. Those types are easy to find. If you've got the money, they've got the time. When Phil finally gets sick of her or when she gets tired of putting up with his temper tantrums— whichever comes first— she'll latch onto the next nearest wallet she can find. You'd better watch yourself, old man. You could be the closest door over. Better you than me, eh!"

I make an attempt to laugh even though I don't consider it to be all that funny. The lack of morals and values evident here is not anything to take pleasure in.

Unaware of my distaste, Rex continues. "Come to think of it, Cloie might just be a little too much for you to handle if you catch my drift." He makes a rather crude bumping motion with his body. "It might be a little too much for your old ticker to take."

He laughs his way over to the couch in the living room and asks me to take a seat. He was preparing dinner when I rang the doorbell, and he needs to check on it. It won't take long. The apartment is laid out in a similar fashion to my own: main living room with attached kitchen, sofa in the center of the room, bedroom and bath located at one end, and patio door to the back garden. Not much different. Maybe his flat is a little more elongated and has a few more personal effects, no doubt because he has lived here for a while and intends to do so for a good while yet—unlike my own situation.

"We are having perch," Rex yells over from the stove where he is frying the fish. He speaks loudly so as to be heard over the sizzling in the pan. "It's good and fresh because I just bought it this morning at the grocery after I found out you had invited yourself to dinner."

Now that joke I do happen to find amusing. There is something about Rex I do in fact like after all. Underneath that layer of crudeness and bad taste, there is still a streak of good humor left untarnished by all the grease he so richly spreads over himself. Before that surprising revelation, I wondered why I had even remotely entertained or, furthermore, agreed to come here tonight. Now I satisfy myself that that had to be the underlying reason. The incident involving Josie had already been laid to rest, and it certainly wasn't just for the free meal. No, there was surely more to it than that. There is something about Rex that leaves me wanting to get to know the man better. He interests me in a way. Maybe it is because he is so different from what I am used to and that makes him kind of appealing. It feels like I am stepping into another world, a world that I have never been a part of. Maybe it is because I need a friend, and he being the only one who offered a hand, I took it. Sometimes even a bad taste in your mouth is better than no taste at all.

"Have you lived here for long?" I ask continuing to dig for information.

By this time Rex has finished slicing the onions, and he begins to pour the wine.

"I moved here about four years ago. It doesn't seem like that long, but I guess it has been four years now since Franny died— since the accident."

"Franny? You mean Francis?" A sick feeling develops in my stomach.

"Yes, Francis."

"What!" I almost choke as the word falls out of my mouth. This hits me as a shock. I am completely stunned. I thought that maybe Brian's sister and Philip had gotten a divorce or something, but I never imagined she was dead. "I didn't know she died. How did it happen?"

Rex seems surprised as well but only for a different reason. "You didn't know? I just assumed you did. You don't mean to say you thought she was still living here with Philip, do you?"

"Well," I feel a little embarrassed by my own ignorance, "I didn't know for sure, but I thought she might."

That seems to slightly amuse Mr. Targent, for his smile slowly stretches from one corner of his lips to the other. He knows I am at a loss. He has me at a loss. He walks over to where I am seated and hands me a glass of wine.

"You poor old bugger. They must really keep you in the dark, don't they?"

I don't know what to say to that. I almost get angry with him yet I also realize

I cannot prove he isn't right. I know he speaks the truth, so I just stay silent.

"Aren't you supposed to be the father-in-law of Franny's brother or something like that? I think that is what Philip said. It's funny that you didn't hear word of it when your son-in-law's sister died— or at least, when you were moving down here."

"I thought I would have too." I am stunned by this realization. Why didn't Brian or Julie mention anything about it? I try to think back. Four years ago? Brian was... No, nothing seemed to point to anything concerning Francis, and Julie never said a thing about it. I know that. I don't know why they would keep it a secret.

"Do you know if Brian, Francis' brother, went to the funeral or not?" I ask.

I half know the answer, for I am pretty sure Brian didn't go anywhere during that time period.

"No, he wasn't there, but I do believe he sent flowers— white roses, I think. Those were her favorites. I remember Philip mentioning that."

It becomes clear to me that this fellow, Rex Targent, knows far more than I do about something I expected him to know very little. I am feeling somewhat angered by apparently being the only one left alone in the dark here. So I call him on it. "You must know Philip Peterson pretty well to know all that?"

"Oh yes, I've known Philip for quite a while. We are no strangers, and we go back a long ways. That is why he asked me here when Franny got sick. He needed someone to help out with running the place— you know, fixing things and taking care of the tenants' needs and that. Looking after Franny took a lot of time and occupied a lot of his attention."

"Sick?" This is yet more news that I have been unaware of. "I thought you said she had an accident."

"She did. She was killed when her car went into the river on the south side of town. She lost control of it and broke through the railing on a corner. It's a particularly bad corner: there have been other accidents on it. The sheriff said she was going too fast. She wasn't in her right frame of mind though. She hadn't been for months. It was some sort of a mental disorder.   The   doctor   had   her   on medication, but it had gotten to the point where she had stopped taking it. She shouldn't have been driving at all. When

Philip wasn't here one morning, she took the keys and left in the car. When Philip got home, he went out looking for her, and it was him who found her. It must have been awful for him. It nearly destroyed him. He blamed himself for what had happened to her. Philip has really changed since then. You wouldn't know it now, but he really loved his wife. She was everything to him. After her death, he didn't know who he was anymore. He's not the same man at all. But as I've said, you wouldn't know it unless you knew him before."

This is a side of Rex I haven't seen before. I have been correct in feeling he is a more decent man than he often lets on- or at least, cares to admit to himself. I had no idea he knew Philip so well, or that he had known Francis, for that matter. Francis was only a name to me, but he had known the person, the woman, the sister- whom Brian never seems to talk about. Still, Brian knows what her favourite flowers were, so they must have been close enough once. What could have happened to cause him to act in such an unnatural manner towards her? Why didn't he go to her funeral? He seems to like Philip well enough. He wasn't so busy back home to prevent him from going: his boss would have given him a few days off. He acknowledged her death by sending the roses. Maybe he didn't see any need to come down here and see her after she died. Maybe all this isn't as odd as I would have myself imagine. The distance that separated them might've been the main reason why they didn't keep in touch and maybe even the reason for him not talking that much about her— as the old saying goes: "out of sight, out of mind." But he does seem to talk about Philip. Maybe he does talk about Francis more than I think. Perhaps it has all just eluded me for some reason. Maybe Brian's and his sister's relationship was completely normal and I am just reading something into it that wasn't even there. I can't remember things like I used to. Maybe I am using these suspicions as some form of security. Maybe I just don't want to admit that there are things in my family's lives that they don't feel the need of letting me in on or talking to me about. It seems that I am not as large a part of it as I thought I was. They have their own lives— their life— and I have mine. Well, I had mine.

I don't know. Perhaps I have just forgotten the times he has mentioned her.

Still, I am sure that Julie would have said something if she knew she had died, and my mind isn't so far gone that I would forget her telling me that. Even if Brian didn't feel the need for it- if he doesn't feel comfortable talking about it- Julie would have surely told me. I think that we are close enough for that. I thought that Brian and I were close enough for that. Why would someone want to keep something like this a secret? He must have known I would find out, anyhow, once I got down here. So why not tell me before? Maybe he didn't think anything of it. Maybe he doesn't think it matters. Maybe it doesn't. Perhaps I am the only one who it really matters to.

This whole thing bewilders me. It would be one thing if I were a complete outsider who just happened to come along and was hearing this information for the first time, then I could simply take it all in as a point of interest. However, when you are directly involved in the storyline and the book you call your life is opened to a chapter and it is revealed to you that a part of that life isn't at all what you have always thought it to be, it starts you wondering what else in your life isn't as it seems and it leaves you not quite knowing how the story will end. I don't know what to think anymore. The next time Julie calls on the phone I will have to ask her if she knows. She has to— unless Brian hasn't told her, either. Rex can see I am having some difficulty taking all this in.

"Don't worry, old man. Some families just aren't that close; they don't talk to each other."

"Maybe you're right," I shrug, "but I always thought we were the type that did."

"Well, maybe that Brian fella is just the sort who tends to keep things bottled up inside. There are those kinds in this world, you do know."

I can see what Rex is doing: he is trying to reassure me I haven't completely lost my mind— not so much out of sincere concern for my well being but more so because the dinner is now ready and he wants to eat it before it gets cold. So I tell him I guess he is right, for I am getting rather hungry myself.

After sitting down in one of the two chairs at either end of the aluminum and ceramic table in the kitchen area— not unlike the one in my own flat— I continue the conversation by noting that "at least Philip still has Josie." I want to know more so that I can try and piece together this mystery which seems to have come out of nowhere. Or perhaps I am the one who has come out of nowhere and has entered into something that is better off left buried. Regardless, I find myself in this place, and now I have a need to know.

"Yes," Rex Targent answers derisively, "he still has Josie," for what that's worth.

He says that kind of slowly, which seems slightly odd.

"Josie and Philip had always been fairly close. She wasn't at all close with her mother, and it only got worse as she got older. That put a lot of stress on Phil. He couldn't stand seeing them not getting along, and he couldn't figure out why they seemed to hate each other so much. Deep down I think he knew, even if he didn't want to admit it. You see, Josie wasn't Francy's. Before Philip and Francis got married, Philip had been very serious about another girl– young woman, I guess, would better describe her. They were even engaged to be married. But then Francy came along. She was a real looker back in those days, and she was interested in Philip. He was quite a catch. He came from a very well-to-do family here in Bronsfield. So Francy set her sights on him even though she knew he was engaged. She didn't care. So really, she shouldn't have complained when she got a little more than she bargained for afterwards. I can't feel sorry for her. You can't really blame Philip for falling for her: I think anyone would have. And fall he did, deeply. He loved Rachel- the other girl- but not like Francis. It was as if she cast a spell over him: he was hers completely. So he broke it off with Rachel and that should have been simple enough. The only trouble was that Rachel was already pregnant. She didn't find out until after Philip had left her. She never told him. If she had, I'm not sure what he would have done. Knowing him, I believe he would have probably done the right thing even if it did tear him apart. But Rachel wasn't the sort of girl who could handle such things. She just sank into herself, and she didn't talk to anyone about it. It wasn't long before her whole mental well being collapsed."

It seems that Philip tends to have that effect on women. I have never really thought about it before, but Brian is also quite good looking and charming in a way too. Perhaps that was what drew Julie to him in the first place. With his dark hair and strong fine features – and knowing his other sister, Darlene – I can see how Francis must have been quite beautiful. But I didn't mean to interrupt. I decide it would be a good idea to pay attention and let Mr. Targent continue– and so he does.

"She had the baby in private. She must have had it all planned out. You do realize that we down South tend to have a terrible fondness for drama, even in our most tragic of circumstances. Oblivious to all that, Philip and Francis went ahead and got married. Back then they were living in a house that Philip's uncle owned over on the south side of town. They returned home from their honeymoon to find a baby in a basket waiting for them on their doorstep. As you can imagine, it was a complete shock for both of them. However, the note that was included with the baby soon cleared matters up in a hurry. It read: 'I know you don't love me anymore but you once did. It was then– in that time– our love came together to create something beautiful. This is her. Take good care of her: she is yours. I will no longer hold onto you. I shall let you go. Be happy in your life. The only thing I ask is for you to remember me. Goodbye

Philip.' She signed it: 'forever yours, Rachel.'

"Now you can imagine how all that must have affected things for the newly married happy couple. It certainly put a damper on their festivities. Both of them were in a state of utter shock. Neither Francis nor Philip had suspected Rachel of being pregnant. At first Francis thought Philip had known and, therefore, accused him accordingly. After all, you couldn't really blame her. Philip swore he had no idea, and after a little convincing, I think she believed him."

"During all that, Rachel must have been nearby quietly observing. She probably just wanted to make sure that they found the baby and to see what happened, maybe to see if it looked as though they would keep the baby. However, I think she already knew Philip would: she knew him. Considering what was about to happen, she wasn't really leaving him with much of a choice. I think she put herself through a lot of unnecessary torture for nothing: she already knew what Philip would do."

"From there she walked to the river and drowned herself. They didn't find her body until the next day. Some local kids were swimming when they came across it. Not the nicest summer afternoon discovery. After finding the baby on their doorstep···. Imagine that! What a way to begin your new life together after arriving home from your honeymoon!"

"Anyhow, they took the baby over to Rachel's mother's house. They hoped that Rachel would be there; although, after reading the note, they thought that maybe she had run off and left town. Even then, they hoped that her mother could make some sense out of the whole situation. When they got there and her mother didn't know where she had gone, it further strengthened their belief she had run away. Her mother had known she was pregnant, and she had even helped to deliver the baby child when the time came. Rachel had refused to go to the hospital. During the pregnancy she had made her mother swear not to tell anyone she was pregnant. She wouldn't even tell her who the father was; although, her mother knew. She knew it was Philip. Even so, knowing the fragile state Rachel was in and not wanting to make things worse, she had agreed to keep quiet. I think she understood how emotionally fragile her daughter really was.

I think she understood because she was a little that way herself."

"After talking to her, Philip and Francy took the baby to the hospital to have it checked over and to make sure it was alright. Not knowing whether or not Rachel had run off somewhere, they weren't sure what to do next. After finding Rachel's body though, it became pretty clear what they were going to do."

"It was a very hard time for both of them⁻ those first few years. Rachel's mother offered to take care of the child but Philip refused. He felt it was his responsibility. He is very serious about things like that. It turns out it was for the best in a way. Rachel's mother was a rather sickly woman⁻ very frail⁻ and if she wasn't finished already, this whole ordeal pretty well did it. It wasn't long after that⁻ maybe a year, maybe two⁻ that she died. So it really was for the best that Philip and Francis had taken the baby. I know that Francis wasn't too keen on the notion, but she did love Philip, and I think she thought it was her duty. I think she always kind of felt in a way that it was her responsibility: she couldn't help but feel a little guilty for what had happened."

"They really struggled with this during the first few years of their marriage. Francis tried to keep her emotions under the surface and put on a brave face, but I think that only made it worse. It was clearly tearing her apart inside. Something like this can destroy a marriage and cause two people to leave one another. I think they were very close to doing so, but they seemed to hang onto each other. They somehow made it through: their love was that strong. I guess they were meant to be together. After that, the pain of it all gradually faded, and I think they actually managed to enjoy a very full marriage – until the tragic ending."

"As it turns out, Josie was a blessing in disguise. For some reason, Philip and Francy were never able to have children of their own and not for want of trying. Francy wanted children very much, very badly. It seems that she believed a child would act as a lasting proof of their love, a proof that Philip and Rachel had already shared but, for some reason, had always eluded her. It was as if it was meant to be, and I believe Francis knew that. She had to live as though Rachel's ghost was always with her. Her ghost hung over her like a black veil. Maybe that was what tore her apart in the end- the constant wearing of Josie on her over the years. I can't help but wonder whether what happened to Francy would have taken place if it hadn't been for Josie. I know it is awful to think, but I can't help but wonder. Rachel's curse has destroyed that whole family."

I feel like I'm being given a rare and privileged view into the Peterson's lives, and I don't want it to stop. Overtop my unease about whether or not I should be hearing such details, I am feeling anticipation for more. I'm finding myself desperately seeking out Rex's next words before they're even spoken, and he continues to speak.

"As Josie gets older, she resembles her mother more and more. She looks very much like her mother. For Philip especially, it must be like looking at a ghost every time he looks at her. He doesn't seem to let it bother him, but I know it does: it has to. When Francy was alive, he was so committed to his love for her that he wouldn't let these emotions surface. After her death, all the years of keeping them buried finally caught up with him and everything just boiled over. But instead of destroying him, it just made him numb. I don't think he feels anything anymore. I don't know if he even loves Josie anymore. I don't know if he ever did— at least, not in the way a father should love his daughter. How can you love something like that? Someone who has destroyed everything you have ever loved. In his eyes, he must see her as an all-consuming force, one that is slowly devouring his very world."

"He was a complete wreck for the first couple of years after Francy's death. Now he at least manages to put up a good front, but it is only a front. Underneath he is nothing but mush. That's why I stay here. Someone has to look after him. Besides, I am the only one who really knows. Cloie doesn't know— or doesn't care to know. She is just a layer of paint upon the shipwreck Philip Peterson has become. Josie can't do anything for him. After all, she is the cause of his bitterness and his pain."

I can't help but wonder how this man, Rex Targent, can be aware of Philip's life in such detail. It is as if he has known him intimately since he was a boy. I say to him, "You must be a very good friend of Philip's."

He answers, "Friends, yes, but we are much more than that. I am the only one who really knows the man. I have known him all his life. I am the only one living who really knows him."

Rex Targent is not as old as me, but he isn't a young man. He looks as though he might be around sixty or so. Philip, on the other hand, even with the hard life he's had, can't be more than forty, and despite the close relationship they seem to share, that age difference makes it rather difficult for me to seriously believe they were childhood friends. Yet who else could be so close through all these years? Could he be his father? That seems to make the most sense. But I'm not going to ask him outright. I am going to let him reveal it to me in his own good time. So he continues.

"For Francis, as the years passed and Josie grew— as she got older— Francis aged tenfold for every year. Her will was just wearing thin. She was crumbling inside, and Josie didn't make it easy on her either. When she was about nine years old, she found out from the other town kids that Francis wasn't her real mother. That was when things really started to unravel. You know how people talk, and it's hard to keep a secret in a small town. It's just as well.

Secrets will destroy you- not unlike so many other things. Yet even before Josie learned this, I think that deep down she knew. She was always closer to her father - daddy's little girl - daddy's only girl. There was a certain friction between her and her mother that couldn't help but exist. And I don't think it was even all Josie's fault. Francis showed a certain coldness towards her. She could never love her - she must never have. After Josie found out though, it only got worse. Resentment grew between them- a kind of hatred. Josie seemed to relish peeling away the layers of Franny's soul and seeing her wilt away before her eyes. What it must have done to her father to watch that. I think she actually enjoyed seeing him suffer. He couldn't do anything about it. He was torn between the two of them, and it was tearing him apart. I swear to God, sometimes I felt like killing her and maybe I should have. I often wish Rachel had drowned that baby right along with herself. It would have eased so much pain - saved so many souls. It was only a matter of time before Francis broke under the enormous weight that had burdened her for so long and crumbled as the dust. It was a relief when she died. At least some of the suffering was eased. It was no accident. When she got into that car, she was running and she wasn't coming back. She had driven right over that railing long before the hot July day she died, and it might as well have been Josie driving the car. So you can see why I have a bad taste in my mouth when it comes to that girl. I truly don't know what will become of her and Philip, I truly don't. If only she would leave, Philip might just stand a chance. I don't know, maybe it's already too late."

I chew my fish and take another sip of wine. I am rather overwhelmed by all Rex has engulfed me in. I came here this evening simply for a meal and a bit of conversation, and I've wound up with more than I bargained for. I wonder why he told me all this. Perhaps he has bottled it up over the years and just wanted to get it off his chest. Maybe I am right- maybe he did. Maybe he chose me because he didn't think I would tell anyone, or last long enough to try. Who am I going to tell? What am I going to tell? Why shouldn't he tell me? After all, I think he is just some crazy neighbor in apartment 1B who's had me in for some fish. It is getting late. He looks tired. He must have stayed up past his bedtime. I am getting tired also. We call it a night.

I leave Rex Targent's apartment full on fish, wine and questions. In spite of everything I have learnt from Rex over dinner, I am still left without rest in my mind. I now know far more than I could have ever possibly comprehended or imagined was lurking under the surface of these lives that inhabit this apartment house with its yellow walls mirroring the sunlight that covers the grayness within. However, it seems that the more questions are answered the more questions arise and ask to be answered. Why has Rex told me all this and in such detail? What exactly is his relationship to Philip Peterson? Is he his father? How can he possibly know so much unless he has been directly involved in their lives? Take the note left with the baby for instance. How can he possibly remember it word for word after all these years? I wonder whether he made at least some of the story up out of his head just for my sake, perhaps to amuse him somewhat. However, certain elements seem to fit. What he told me would make sense out of a lot of things; although I still don't know why Josie apparently goes by the name of Spencer. Maybe it was her mother's last name and she has taken to calling herself by that name just to spite her father. That would certainly make sense if the rest of the story is true. I have no real reason to believe it is not, so until proven otherwise, I will have to accept it at face value and take Rex Targent's word for it.

But the question remains there refusing to go away. Why, if Philip wants to bury this dark family secret and somehow attempt to deny its existence, did Rex, who is supposedly very close to Philip, go and pour it out so freely like sugar out of a jar to a practical stranger? Even though I do possess remote ties to the family, it still doesn't make much sense. My questions can simply and easily be answered by a basic version of the truth. That will suitably satisfy me. It is almost as if he wants me to know. He needs me to become entrapped by the secret also. He feels the need to pull me into its midst and make me a part of it as if I myself have a part to play in this. Only, I do not know what that part is to become.

Other questions swirl around my weary mind as I prepare for bed. Why did Josie develop such hatred towards Francis and at such a young age? I can understand how a sore spot might have developed once Josie found out that Francis wasn't her real mother, but to believe Josie would cause her stepmother such pain and suffering over it to the point that it would drive Francis towards a mental breakdown is almost beyond me. After all, Francis was the mother who had raised and taken care of her. You would expect Josie would feel some sort of closeness to her. It just doesn't make sense to me. How can you hate someone so much because of something you have never known? Perhaps Francis caused her own misery: out of guilt, she brought her downfall upon herself. Maybe her hatred for Josie caused Josie, in turn, to hate her stepmother. Josie was too strong a reminder of the bond that Philip and Rachel had shared. Francis knew that she and Philip would never have the same bond no matter how strong their love was for one another. Perhaps she also saw herself as the imposter in their lives who had brought about all this misery. What if it was Philip and Rachel who were meant to be together? Did she destroy their chance for happiness? Even the smallest grain of guilt can wear away at a person until it destroys them entirely.

I don't know how you can blame Josie for that. I can't believe Josie would do that to the woman who had rocked her to sleep at night as a baby, caught her when she was about to fall while taking her first steps, and held her in her arms when she awoke crying in the dark of night.

Sleep comes softly, and I rest.

CHAPTER 8

THE STOCKY MAN

I awake at 3:00 a.m. My bladder has alerted me to the need for a bathroom visit. I used to be able to make it through an entire night without such an inconvenience. Now, however, this nightly ritual has become routine. As I stand over the bowl trying not to dribble on the floor, my eyes squint attempting to adjust to the light emanating from the bulb on the ceiling. The tile floor is cold beneath my bare feet. I hasten my task, for I want to return to my cozy bed as soon as possible. Even with the warm climate down here, it still manages to get surprisingly cool at this time of night. I guess it has something to do with it being November. They have to have some form of winter down here as well.

As I walk back to my bedroom, I wonder how I made it through the previous night without my bladder exploding. I must not have drunk very much.

When I return to my bed, I notice a light on across the square in Rex Targent's apartment. That's odd. You wouldn't think that he would still be up at this time of night. Maybe he can't sleep. I have always noticed that people who tend to talk an awful lot quite often are kind of nervous, and nervous people usually have trouble sleeping. I am fortunate that I've never had that problem myself. After ten or fifteen minutes in bed, I am out like a light until morning– or at least, until my bladder comes a knockin' on the door to my dream world like tonight.

I go over to my window and close the screen. A cool breeze is blowing in, and it gives me a bit of a chill. My sleepy eyes squint through the window glass. I see some movement, so I focus my vision. My eyes are not as good as they used to be, but at least I don't have to wear glasses. I can make out two men standing in Rex's living room. One of them is Rex. I don't know who the other one is. I haven't seen him before. They appear to be arguing about something. They sure seem to be an argumentative bunch around here: nobody seems to be able to get along. But what could be so important that it would trigger a row at this time of night? I find it strange how they are not in their pajamas or night clothes– or even in their underwear like I am right now. Instead, they are fully clothed. Rex still has on the shirt and pants he wore last night. Has he not slept at all? There appears to be someone else in the room with them as well. I can make out a shadow cast by the lamplight on the floor and moving about the room. Every so often, the two men turn in the direction of the shadow as if talking to someone there. The other person enters my range of view. It is Philip. The three of them seem to be in a heated discussion. Philip is pacing the floor, and Rex looks as though he is trying to convince the other man of something, but the other man isn't agreeing. Philip stops in front of the window and stands there looking out. His face is flush from the argument, but he also has a worried look about him. I hope he doesn't see me here standing in the window watching. My heart pounds – until he turns away again. He had me worried. However, with the light off in my room and the light on over there, it is unlikely he saw anything but the pitch blackness of night.

I continue to observe them from the safety of my darkened room. They go on bickering amongst themselves for several more minutes before disappearing from view. Then the light goes off and I can see no more. There are no lights on in the bedroom or in the bathroom, either. I am about to return to my bed figuring the show now over when I notice the screen door to the back of Rex's flat open. A figure steps out. They proceed to walk across the square before opening the back door of the flat directly parallel with Rex Targent's on the other side of the courtyard. They step inside and close the door behind. A light comes on in a few seconds. Through the window I can see it is the other man from Rex's apartment who was involved in the argument. He has to be my other neighbour. They are certainly a neighborly bunch – coming over to one another's and yelling at three... I check my clock... 3:21 in the morning. I wondered who lived there.

The man is a relatively short and stocky sort with dark gray hair and sideburns. He is an older man. He looks to be in his sixties as near as I can tell. It is the norm for this place. The tenants are made up for the most part of retirees. I figure that is likely the case because Phil knows we are less trouble and regular with the rent. There is also, apparently, an unending supply of us. The light in the apartment I now have under my observation goes out in a few moments. Another light comes on just briefly in another room, which I take to be either the bedroom or bathroom, before going out as well. Hmm. I wonder what the argument could have been about. There appears to be so much more going on around this place than at first would meet the eye. I have been delivered into a real hornets nest down here. This is supposed to be a peaceful time for me. I am supposed to be idling my days away under the shade of the willow trees with nothing more on my mind than what kind of jello I am to have for dessert. I am not supposed to be staring out the window in the middle of the night worrying about what ungodly thing is hatching in my neighbor's apartment. Yet, here I am. I will be better off if I return to bed. I can close my eyes and try to forget I ever saw a thing. I think it best to just go and do that. Before long, I manage to fall back to sleep.

I awake to the sound of birds chirping outside my window. I determine that there is a nest in the wall above my window, for I can hear a scratching and rustling sound coming from that area. At first I thought it might be rats in the wall, but by now I have pretty much ruled that out. The more I listen the more I am sure it is birds. I am very much relieved by that. I wasn't altogether comfortable with the idea that my walls were the breeding grounds for those filthy rodents. I am not particularly fond of rats. I have seen enough of them in my day. I know the diseases they can carry and the damage they can do to a home, and I have seen some big ones too- ones so big that they were the size of a cat. When the cats would see them, the cats would just run. When you would see them climbing up a wall, their tails looked like snakes. It sends a shiver down my spine when I think of them creeping around the floor and crawling over my bed while I am sleeping at night. Rats disgust me!

Birds, on the other hand, I like. I lie in bed listening to their chatter. I sigh and look at the clock. It is 6:45 a.m. and time to get up. However, there isn't any big rush. It doesn't matter what time I get up now. I don't have a lot to do other than sit around, anyhow.

This relaxed way of life is going to take some time getting used to. I have always been a fairly early bird. Even after I retired, there were still plenty of jobs around the house to keep me busy. Maybe the trouble is that I don't really have any hobbies. It used to be that work and my family took up the lion's share of my time. After that, any free time was spent on the house. There was so much to do with the house. I did most of the work myself, and I put a lot into it. The house was sort of like a hobby for me. Now it is sitting back home and I am here finding I no longer have a thing to do. I never thought that I would have this problem. Then again, I don't think about very much anymore. All I know is that they wanted me to move down here. They seem to be doing the rest of my thinking for me. Well, they haven't thought of this. What am I supposed to do down here, wait to die? Maybe they think I am dead by now. Well, I am not! I have to find something to occupy my time. Going on like this, any man would be dead before long. Hmm, but what am I interested in? What do other people my age do to keep busy? Lawn bowling, bingo, shuffleboard, bus trips come to mind– all rather uninteresting excursions, to say the least. As for travel, just coming here was plenty enough travelling for me to have had my fill of it already. Besides, riding around on a bumpy bus and being herded from place to place like a bunch of sheep isn't exactly my idea of a rip-roaring good time. No, what I need is something I can really sink my teeth into- or my dentures, at the very least.

What was it that I used to enjoy doing? There was always something purposeful in my life that needed doing, and I went and did it and that was that. When I was a boy, I used to enjoy baseball but even that had its purpose in the time. Now I can no more play it than... and I don't think I would even enjoy it anymore. Perhaps the only thing purposeful left in my life that is in need of doing is dying. Maybe I am better to get on and do it then and be done with it. Ha! That is kind of funny. I don't know what I enjoy doing anymore. Ah, the plight of the old man. I just don't know.

Maybe I need a job. I am too old for a job. Who would hire me? Even if they did, I would probably just go and die on them anyhow, and that would be about it.

Another thing is that I don't really know this place very well at all. Maybe I will go and ask Rex. Perhaps he knows of some good things to do. He seems to be able to keep himself suitably preoccupied helping Philip around the place; although, last night he didn't appear to be helping Phil out too much‾ at least, not in the conventional sense of the word. Maybe I can help too.

I have managed to put last night's events out of my mind until now when it all comes flooding back to me. I wonder whether I have dreamt it all, the result having come from too much fish and wine the night before, but I am pretty certain I haven't. I was awake well enough last night to now remember it clearly and in detail: the pacing of the room, the red frustrated faces, the stocky man walking to his flat across the courtyard, the worried look on Philip Peterson's face. It is all as clear as day.

Hmm, now that is something I want to do: find out what has been going on over there and, maybe, get to know my other neighbor a little bit. I'm not going to let on I saw them, but maybe Rex will be only too good to tell me all about it. Maybe he needs to get this off his chest too. Perhaps he just needs a little encouragement and a friendly ear to be made available to him. Yes, now I do have something to do‾ at least for today. I will have to pay my good pal Rex a visit‾ after I have eaten some breakfast and unpacked another suitcase. Yes, that is what I will have to do.

I arise from my comfortable bed and comfortable it is. My bed back home, which I spent a good part of my life sleeping in, would be hard pressed to compare. I grew so used to its peculiar bumps and hollows that I never really thought about it; my body sort of adapted to suit. As with so much in life, things are rarely a perfect fit; you have to mold together for things to work. After sleeping in this bed for a couple of nights though, I realize that it is very comfortable indeed. That is one good thing about this place. Well, there are others, of course. For instance, one would be hard pressed to find a better view than this simply wonderful delight right outside my window.

I gaze out upon the sunlit garden scene. Little birds with yellow breasts are splashing about in the stone-carved birdbath below. The sun's warmth penetrates my skin and warms my heart. My eyes fall on Josie's bare skin. She is there again lying naked on her stomach, backside exposed to the sun and to any onlookers who might be aroused early in the morning. My glance shoots over to Rex Targent's window. No, he isn't watching. No sign of Rex. He must still be asleep after that late night of his. Maybe she lies out there on every nice day. Perhaps it has become a regular routine for her. Maybe Rex is right‑ she has no shame. She has to know somebody is bound to see her sometime. Maybe she likes the way people watch. Perhaps everything Rex said about her is true: she is no angel. Of course, from the first time I talked to her, on the first day I arrived here, I could have told you that. But who would have known that sweet little girl would turn out to harbor so much evil within her?

Evil. What is evil‑ someone who takes pleasure in sin? Then half the world would be evil. Someone who takes pleasure in the misery and suffering of others‑ maybe that is evil. But what if you are thrown into an environment‑ out of no free will of your own‑ that breeds pain and hatred and you are subjected to it on a daily basis? If you are raised into it, what else is to come from it? Is it not natural for you to hate those who show hatred towards you if you have never known anything else? Everyone protects themselves in different ways. Sometimes, to protect yourself, you destroy others even if you do love them.

I don't know if I can blame Josie for what she has become. If I am to hate her for it, am I myself not evil? After all, she is just a girl– a lost, little girl. If what Rex says is true– and I am beginning to believe it might well be, from what I have seen so far– I feel sorry for her more than anything. I feel sorry for us all.

CHAPTER 9

A HARD ACT TO FOLLOW

A knock on my door takes hold of my attention. I wonder who that could be at this time of the morning. Shit! I have an erection⁻ you filthy old bastard you. I didn't think that I could get these anymore. I can't remember the last time I've had one. This is supposed to be another thing that fades with old age. Well, it is a great time to have one now with somebody at the door. The knocking continues. I get my pants on and pull a sweater on over my head. It is still hard. I am trying to get the sick thoughts out of my head. They aren't leaving fast enough. What am I going to do now? I am attempting to think of all the most unattractive repulsive things I can imagine.

"Hello, anybody in there?"

The voice is a woman's. That is just great. If I go out there like this, she will probably have me charged for sexual harassment. I notice my suit jacket hanging on the closet door. Good, if I am to put that on, button it up and make a few adjustments, it should cover me and she shouldn't be able to tell. I put the jacket on and go to the door and answer it. On the other side I am greeted by a middle aged, somewhat out of breath, rather attractive woman. She seems a little exasperated about having to knock so long for me to answer. Before she even introduces herself, I figure her for who she is. She has on nothing more than a plush bathrobe and a pair of furry high heeled slippers, yet she has still managed to take the time to don some make-up and brush her hair even though it is clearly evident she has just awakened. The sort of woman she is is written all over her and the only one who fits that description whom I know of is Cloie, Philip Peterson's apparent live-in companion. Yes, and that is exactly who it is.

"I'm Cloie," she says. "There's a phone call for you. It's from your daughter. Philip isn't here, so I had to take it."

She seems clearly inconvenienced by the whole ordeal.

"She's on the line right now. If you want to speak to her, then I'm suggesting you come up with me."

Of course I want to speak to her. I put on my shoes and follow her right up. She is certainly in a cranky mood. I guess that she isn't a morning person, or maybe she just doesn't appreciate being disturbed from her beauty sleep by the ringing of the phone. Then it only got worse from there. When her Philip was nowhere to be found to answer it, she had to march down to some damn old tenant's apartment and bang on the door. It must have seemed like half an hour before I finally opened it. Yes, that probably hits the nail right on the end of the hammer. Surely that is why she appears to be fuming as she silently leads me up to her flat without so much as a word of encouragement. I can clearly see how she and Philip might come to argue from time to time. I bet she wishes that all of us apartment dwellers in the building had phones of our own right now. I am also quite certain that Philip will come to hear her complaint— most probably the very next time the two should merge. Quite truthfully, despite Philip's reasoning for having this system in his building, I cannot help but think it to be at least a tad bit unpractical— not so much for the tenants but more so for the landlords.

We get up to the flat. Cloie points towards the phone in the midst of the living room, and then she returns to what I figure to be her bedroom. Their flat is not laid out the same as the others I have been in- those being my own and Rex Targent's. There are more separated rooms. For instance, the kitchen is not an addition to the living room. I was correct in my earlier assumption, for it appears that the Peterson's flat takes up the whole upstairs level of the building. The central living room stretches all the way from the front of the building to the patio overlooking the square below with rooms along both sides of the living room. The two wings along the sides of the courtyard seem to each be made up of one big room. The one directly above Rex Targent's apartment looks to be a bedroom. The door is open, and I can see a bed and some clothes scattered about on the floor. It is most likely Josie's room, for there are some posters stuck on the walls and some panties and a brassiere hung over the end of the bed- and they look too small to be Cloie's. She is a shapely woman but certainly not petite.

The thought comes over me that Josie might come up the courtyard stairs while I am standing here in the living room talking on the phone. She is still out there. I hope she doesn't. I don't know what I will do. Perhaps, if I turn the other way and pretend I don't notice her − that will be the best idea. I don't think she will deliberately try and draw attention to herself to get me to look, but you never know with her. I think it best to talk quickly and get out of here as fast as I can. I wonder if her mother knows. Oh, that's right, Cloie is not her mother, but I wonder if she knows Josie lies out there like that. I don't see how she cannot. However, from what I have heard of Cloie, she probably wouldn't think anything wrong with it. I am a little surprised that she is not out there herself trying to attract flies to honey. I suppose that she has her fly entrapped already. I wonder if Philip knows his daughter lies out there like that.

If he does, I don't know how he can put up with it. It is disgraceful. What kind of a father is he? It is sick. He has a certain responsibility as her father. If my daughter were to try something like that, I wouldn't stand for it for one minute.

Julie. Shoot! She has been waiting a long time. Who knows how long she has been on the line, especially if she was waiting the entire time it took Cloie to get herself sufficiently dolled up to come down and get me. At least, I don't imagine Cloie sleeps with her make-up on. Anyhow, it has to be costing her a fortune.

"Hello. Hello, dear, it's your father."

CHAPTER 10

HOMESICK BLUE

My voice sounds meek and crackly like an old man's. Her father is an old man. She sometimes forgets that. She doesn't want to see me like this: it makes her sad. Julie knows she has to be strong. She doesn't want me to hear her crying, for she doesn't want to worry me.

"Hello, dad, how are you? Getting settled in alright down there? Are you doing okay? When I called yesterday and didn't get you, I thought I had better try you again- earlier in the morning this time- just to make sure you had gotten there alright and had gotten yourself settled in."

I try to sound cheerful and put on a brave face, but she knows how I really feel. I don't want to be here, and I blame her for forcing me to go. She didn't have to send me. She could've looked after me there if she wanted to. If she wasn't so selfish, if she really loved me, she would've never made me go to some God-forsaken place that was all strange and unfamiliar to me. At this stage in my life, I shouldn't have to go through that. I should be around the people who love me and will look after me. I should be in my home with my family around me. A good daughter wouldn't do that to her father no matter what anybody said was for the best. She would know what was for the best.

My voice is soothing; she feels like my little girl all over again. When she used to come running to me in tears, I would sit her on my knee and hold her in my arms− those strong safe arms. I would always reassure her that the world was not coming to an end, and I would take my handkerchief and wipe those tears away. I am doing it again.

I tell her I arrived here safely without any major problems and have gotten myself settled in. She and Brian made all the arrangements. Even the first month's rent was paid in advance, so it has been "smooth sailing", as I so characteristically put it. I tell her I might get to like it down here and not want to go back home or leave at all, so they had better watch out. I have even made a new friend. If I managed to fool her up until now with this cloak of enjoyment I cast over her− its texture so sweet and so thin−

the reassuring light is beginning to dim. She knows her father, and she knows I do not tend to make friends easily. That is just how I am. I am my own man, and my family is my life. I never leave a place close to me reserved for others. That is just who I am− the kind of man I am. It is not at all like me to make a new friend so quickly− if she believes me capable of making friends at all. So she can see it is all only a slim disguise for the sake of her feelings. I want to make her feel secure and protected. How she loves me. How can she turn away from me− not now when I need her the most?

It is only to be for the winter, and then I will return home. That was what they told me. She doesn't know if I believe it. She doesn't know if they believe it themselves.

What I say next catches her completely off guard. She is about to close off the conversation content in the knowledge I am settled in just fine and relieved that the stress from the whole ordeal hasn't caused me to take a turn for the worse. She wanted reassurance and that was what I so unselfishly gave her. Just hearing my voice has made her homesick for me− as much as she knows that I am for them. She wants to hang up the phone before she gives in to herself and begs me to come back home. She is about to whisper I love you and take care always when I say it.

"Francis is dead. Did you know Brian's sister was dead?"

There was no build up- not even the slightest little hint that I was about to change the course of the conversation towards those three words: Francis is dead. At first, Julie thinks I mean she has just died, and she is sort of in a state of shock and remorse. She didn't know her personally. Francis and Brian never saw that much of one another.

Brian told her that Francis had left home when she was quite young- just 16- and she had never really made an attempt to keep in touch. Francis had carved out a life of her own down in Georgia. Sure, there was the odd Christmas card home with a brief note saying she was well. Brian's parents took it very hard. They couldn't believe she would just up and leave and then practically disown her family- shutting them out of her life the way she did. Brian never really understood it. He'd gotten used to it, though. It was just the way Francis was. If she wanted to keep her family at a distance, there wasn't really much that they could do.

Brian used to write her letters asking her why she never came home to visit or kept in touch more often. She never answered him– not even once. He wasn't sure if she had even received the letters. All he had to go by were old addresses on the backs of envelopes from the few Christmas cards she had sent. They knew she was living in Georgia, but her address had changed from time to time over the years. They knew she had left home in search of a singing career– of all things– but that was it. They didn't know if she'd found what she was searching for or what kind of a job she had. They didn't really know anything about her life at all. But that didn't change because of Francis.

It was only after Francis had married Philip that her family found out how she was doing. It was Philip who made an effort to get to know and to keep in touch with his wife's family. He started to write. It was through Philip's efforts that they first learned she had gotten married. For a while there, he was writing to them every second month telling them about how he and Francis were doing. It was as though he wanted to feel closer to his wife through her family. He would ask all kinds of questions about her childhood, and he wanted to know what she had been like growing up. He took a very strong interest in his wife's life. Francis' parents were relieved she had married someone who obviously cared about her so much. You can imagine how grateful they were to have a son-in-law making such an effort to bring their daughter back into their lives and it all happened so fast. Philip even invited them to come down and visit and to stay with them. Her parents could've been reunited with their daughter once again. Brian could've seen for himself how his little sister had grown into a woman. It could have been a happy reunion if only Francis would've asked them herself. She never did. Even though her family was on friendly terms with Philip, if Francis did not want them there, there was no sense in going.

Brian had often thought of going down there and visiting them sometime. Philip had left an open invitation, but it was always Francis who stood in the way. Brian had hoped that would change someday. He always sent Philip and

Francis a Christmas card at Christmas, and Philip sent one to them every year. It used to be that Francis would write a short note at the bottom of the card. She didn't even take the time to sign the last few cards herself. Philip wrote out the cards, and he signed them: "from Philip & Francis". Instead of becoming closer, it seemed that Brian and Francis were drifting even further apart.

Julie doesn't talk much to Brian about Francis anymore. She knows he prefers not to talk about it. His family has become the same way. They acknowledge her life, but it ends there. They have their life, and she has hers. They always leave a place in their lives open for her. It is Philip who resides there now. If you leave a window open long enough, sooner or later a bird is going to fly in.

"Francis is dead."

Those words take their time to sink in. "When did that happen?" She asks me. She cannot help but feel a sense of remorse. Now Brian will never be able to come to terms with his sister. She had always held onto the hope that things between them would change someday. Now that hope is gone, and she feels a deep loss in her heart. As my words become clearer, she suddenly becomes aware of a sickening feeling all over her body. It is as if oil were slowly soaking into her skin.

"She died in an accident about four years ago."

"Four years ago."

She realizes I think she knew.

"Brian knew: he sent flowers for her funeral. He must have told you."

Maybe Brian hasn't told her.

"Why didn't you tell me?" I ask. "I felt rather foolish when I had to explain that I didn't know Philip's wife was dead. It looked as though nobody told me anything. I felt kind of stupid."

She feels kind of stupid as well. Her husband has failed to inform her of his own sister's death. Why hasn't Brian told her? Talking about Francis might be something he is not comfortable with, but why in God's name would he not tell her this? She just can't believe he wouldn't tell her something of this importance. If she had known, they would have gone to the funeral. Francis was his sister, after all. She can hardly believe what she is seeing – this side of her husband. She had no idea that Francis played so powerful a role in her husband's life. Has he done such a good job of hiding it from her?

I thought she knew: just as she feels she should have known herself. I feel outside, alone, and betrayed. She knows what I am feeling: she is feeling it for herself. The picture is beginning to become clearer for me that she too has been kept in the dark on this matter. The relief I gain from that knowledge also brings with it a new form of uneasiness. I can hear in her voice that she is deeply troubled by my unrest. She wanted to leave me feeling reassured after our conversation, and she wanted to leave herself reassured as well. That was the whole point of this telephone call. She wanted it to be like a warm hug – comforting to us both. Instead, now I am worrying for her more than ever. My little girl is crumbling right before my eyes, and I know that there is little that I can do. I wish I hadn't said anything. I could have protected her from the truth. We could have gone on living with the sun shining clouding out what lay beyond the horizon. When you believe everything is alright, isn't it? Isn't it better than when you know it is not? She tries to explain away Brian's reasons for not telling her. It would have to have caused him great pain.

I listen to her uncertainty. She isn't sure who is more at a loss. She attempts to assure me that there is some reasonable explanation for Brian's behaviour. I attempt to reassure her that she believes what she is saying to me. Before our talk comes to an end, I say I love her- and she knows I do- and she feels a little better. She lets me know that she loves me too.

The phone receiver clicks down with a hollow echo. I find myself standing here unable to move. What have I done? I thought she knew. How could I be so selfish? I didn't even consider the consequences of her not knowing then finding out this way. I just assumed she knew. The last thing I ever wanted to do was cause grief. Now what have I gone and done? I regret even saying a word.

Why didn't Brian tell her? Why did he have to go and make things so hard? Why did he not simply tell Julie? He must have had his reasons. Francis was his sister, after all. Perhaps it was too personal. It was so difficult for him to comprehend that he couldn't even share it with his own wife. It is his grief, no other's– not hers nor mine– his alone. The depth to it might well be endless. If Brian did not want to tell her– if he could not tell her– then who was I to do it? I'm her father. It was Brian's secret, not mine. This is his doing; it is his responsibility to mend what has been broken. I hate the part that I have to play in it all. I only hope things can find a way of healing themselves. I feel as though I've been sleep–walking and have awakened unsure of where I am or what I have just done.

CHAPTER 11

THE NAKED CORPSE

Immersed deeply in my worries, I did not give much notice to Cloie leaving her room, walking past me and going out the patio door. After putting down the receiver, I have been standing here in a daze. I am attempting to come to grips with all that has just happened.

The scream from the square below breaks me out of the grip I have been clenched in like a sledgehammer breaking through a block of ice. My mind quickly pieces together the events that have just transpired without my realization. Cloie is out in the back garden. She must have seen Josie. Maybe she hasn't been aware of some of the things Josie has been doing. It sounds like it must have given her quite a shock, for she does not scream just once but again and again. It does not sound as though she has merely been given a surprise. It sounds like.... I hurry over to the patio door. It is Cloie alright. She's hysterical. She has her hands on the sides of her head. She is shrieking over and over again. The sound makes the hair on the back of my neck stand up. She is standing over Josie's lawn chair. When I get to the doorway, I half expect to see Josie's naked body come running up the stairs to the safety of her own room. Perhaps she can hide out until the storm has blown over. I am starting to feel uneasy about how I will react to having her run right past me on her way to her room. However, that is not happening. Josie is still lying face down on the chair. One arm is dangling over the side; the other is resting at her side. She is not moving. If she is simply asleep, she will surely be awakened by the screams. It is beginning to register in my head that something is not right here.

Rex Targent comes out of his apartment still dressed in his undershirt and shorts. He goes over to Josie and shakes her trying to wake her. The horrible realization that has begun to creep its way over me reaches its peak. As Rex releases her, Josie's body slumps lifeless over the edge of the chair. Her head turns towards me revealing her eyes wide open and staring straight through me. Her gaze is fixed and unchanging. There is nothing behind those eyes. The bright light, which resided there as near as only yesterday, has dulled and gone away. The hollow glow that hangs there now is not even death. Its shadow has already gone and left behind... only emptiness. The image of those black eyes staring – endlessly gaping at me as if in question to their fate – is mine to keep. I know right here that this picture will never leave me. For as long as I shall live, it will stay with me and haunt me for an eternity. It will be a constant, ever present reminder, never passing away – not completely – for it now resides here and thus it will remain.

Rex stares in horror at Josie's lifeless form slumped in front of him. I can imagine how he must still feel her cold flesh in his hands as if he were still holding her. He looks as though he is about to be sick. He fights to hold it back. He looks over at Cloie who is still caught in the grip of hysterics. Then his eyes travel to where I am standing– on the Peterson's patio at the head of the stairs overlooking the scene. For an instant, I think he has a look of worry on his face as if some sort of an unexpected realization has just come over him. His face drains of all color to match the girl's lying there beneath him. I'm not sure whether his thoughts cause him to react in such a manner or whether it is simply an effect from the shock of the entire situation. His eyes quickly look away again.

By this time Cloie's screams have managed to arouse the entire building. The stocky man, who I saw the night before, comes out of his flat and into the square. He looks equally disturbed. He attempts to calm Cloie down. At first she seems reluctant to accept, but she soon gives in and throws herself into his arms taking comfort, sobbing bitterly. This display of hers – is it just that – simply a show? Is she only acting the part of the grieving mother figure? I don't think that she has ever even pretended to assume that role. So why does she make all this fuss now? Perhaps the sheer depth and tragedy of the horror which awaited her discovery this morning is simply too much for her to bear. It could become due cause for such a response. More so, and much more plausible an explanation, than if her hysterics are taken to be considered for being but an outer sign of the inner destruction taking place at this time in secrecy– all bore out of the loss⋯ for deep love of this child. How can she love her in that way? After witnessing everything this woman appears to be, her response is very hard to believe.

I am joined on the upper terrace by an elderly man and woman. They are followed by a little, stooped lady. She looks to be about 90. She leans on a cane for support, and I am rather impressed that she even managed to climb the stairs to the Peterson's flat. This reminds me of something Josie said to me on the first day I arrived– something about me not having to worry about climbing any stairs. If this old lady can do it, well, I think that I should be able to manage. I remember telling her something to that nature as well.

The three had come up that way upon hearing the screams. The man informs me that they are the other tenants who live in the two front corner apartments on the lower floor of the building. We quickly introduce ourselves – both briefly as the situation does not warrant more elaborate courtesies. They are Mr. and Mrs. Loiselle. The older woman lives alone in the other apartment, and the man informs me that her name is Mrs. Snoden. When Mrs. Loiselle sees the scene down below, she becomes very concerned. It is a strange mixture of shock and genuine sadness, which I have found overcomes most women when they witness something tragic. My wife used to get that way when she would read about an accident or death in the newspaper.

Mrs. Loiselle's husband comforts her and takes her into the Peterson's flat. There is no need to look any further. It is clear they are shocked not only by what they have just seen but by the surprise of something like this happening in their own building and to someone whom they have obviously known well. It is both a reaction of overwhelming disbelief and a painful realization of loss. Philip said that Josie ran a lot of errands for the people who lived in the building and also spent a lot of time with them.

For the man's wife− and for Cloie to a similar extent− it is not only the initial shock of unexpected tragedy. It is more a matter of being torn apart emotionally − of not being able to understand − not only why but how something so horrific in nature could have possibly taken place. How could a life so young and with such promise be snatched away in an instant? It is as though the balance in their world has been broken. Perhaps in this moment they understand how vulnerable and fragile their lives really are. What greater horror could one come to realize? Even though Cloie is a relative newcomer to the Peterson household, the time that she spent living with Josie must have brought about some form of emotional attachment. After all, she supposedly loves Josie's father. Operating under that premise, it seems only reasonable to expect she would become close to his daughter as well. Despite what Rex says about the kind of girl he thinks Josie to be and the extent of Cloie's relationship to Philip, the fact remains; the three would not have been together if there was not something keeping them there. When you spend time close to others, it is only logical to assume that some sense of a bond will be formed. And when that part is taken away, you can't help but feel a certain loss. It is only reasonable to expect that Cloie would experience just such a loss. She is a very emotional person and that might be the reason for her strong reaction. It is not unreasonable to assume. Wouldn't anyone who was close to someone and came upon them that way react in a similar fashion? Would it not be unnatural if they did not?

Mrs. Snoden seems to be having difficulty seeing what is down below her. I observe that she is standing very close to the balcony railing near the stairs trying to squint through her thick rimmed glasses. I wonder if she even knows what is going on. If she does not, she is better off for it. She does not need to see this. I think I had better take her back into the apartment before she falls down the stairs, for she looks very unsteady and is dangerously close to the top of the stairway. In fact, her cane, which she seems to count on for a good deal of her support, is resting right on the edge of the top stair's ledge. If she loses her balance, she will fall down the stairs.

"Mrs. Snoden, why don't we go back inside and..?" Just as I am about to make a grab for her arm, she spins around towards me so quickly that it startles even me. The sudden sound of my voice has given her a scare. I must have spoken directly into her hearing aid. She spins so quickly that her cane slips off the step- as I was afraid of- causing her to stumble backwards. I grab for the old lady's arm in a frantic attempt to catch her before she topples over the railing. The horror seizes me, for instead of grasping her arm my fingers only dig into the soft cloth of her dressing gown. I grasp it tightly in my clenched fist, but the old lady continues to fall backwards. She lets out a terrible scream as if she knows the fate that awaits her at the foot of the stairs. As she screams, her eyes dig into me begging to be spared. They follow me as the dressing gown tears away from her withered body revealing her naked flesh. I stare helplessly as her body thumps against the top of the railing and then rolls over the edge of the staircase and plunges to the stone walk below. Her body hits the stone with a smack. It resembles the sound given off by a swat to the fleshy part of someone's arm or leg. Her scream does not last all the way down. It ends about halfway down as if she knew of the outcome and had accepted it.

Her body lies motionless now. All is still and deadly quiet. All who are there stop and stare. There is no sobbing to be heard. No birds are singing. A cloud moves over the sun, and the sky becomes a pale gray. Out of all the ways I have seen or imagined a body falling, none of it has prepared me for this sight. The way she fell was unlike anything I thought possible. You can't see her head. It is bent completely under her chest. As she lies front down on the flat stone below, a small pool of red begins to form underneath her.

I can hear Cloie's voice uttering, "Oh my God." She is no more than 20 feet away, but it seems like I am outside the scene. Everything is at a distance. I am standing at the top of the stairs still clutching her dress in my hand. I cannot relax my grip on it. My fingernails dig into the flesh of my palm. I can only stare at the pale white form on the stone framed with red.

The other voices are emitting words. They have stirred from their frozen state of initial shock. To me it is only a buzz in my ears. I cannot distinguish or make out what they are saying or what is being said. In my head, I remain still looking into those eyes. I was the last to see her soul before she was to leave. I saw death hovering over her and then entering in when it saw its chance. What I saw was pure terror in her eyes. Her soul did not want to leave. If I have ever thought dying might be a pleasant passing, after having just looked death in the face, I see it now only to be misery. She saw what lay ahead for her, and the light did not embrace her; it terrified her. It was not what awaited her when she hit the ground below; it was what was waiting for her afterwards that she found disturbing.

I was the last thing those eyes were ever to see. As they locked onto mine, it felt as though they were pulling my soul away along with hers. In that moment I could see into her soul and I was just as sure that she could see into mine and that death would see us both. I was the final glimpse of life she was ever to have, and she did not want to let it go. She would have pulled me down with her unwilling to release the only thing she could latch onto. Her eyes tried to pull my soul through mine and into hers- to follow where she was heading. She wouldn't have let go, for she blamed me. I was the architect of her death. I stood here and opened the door and watched as death entered in. I was the cause of her destruction, and in her eyes, I should have followed her fate. She was drowning, and she would have pulled me down with her. I cannot blame her. She couldn't see I was trying to save her. All she saw was leaving- becoming dim. In the hollow light that remained was all that she had lost. Within a shadow of the crow, she saw death, and it blurred with my likeness. Within her pain, I was the last to remain.

She is gone. I stand here trembling. Everything around me becomes vivid.

Cloie's red V-neck sweater flashes so brightly in the sunlight that it is almost blinding. The grey hairs on Rex Targent's head stand out as though they are under a microscope's glass. The stocky man's voice booms hollow and clear. "What happened?" it echoes. I can hear cars in the street a block away as if they are right outside the building. The crickets in the grass in the garden below are clear as crystal in my ears. The pool of blood is as red as the dark of night. Her skin is so white, like picket fence board in July. I can see a bird upon the sky a mile south and twice as high. As black as pain are wings that fly.

It is as though a switch has been turned on in my head; like the volume has been turned up and the picture made clear; as if a television set were coming on with a crisp click out of what was only dull static before. My soul has returned to me. I am not willing to let it go just yet. In death she had to release me. It is not my time; death will have to wait for me. As it was pulled away from me, life now pours back into my veins. As it dulled, my spirit now shines brightly with a renewed force. As I fell, I now arise.

I stand here on my perch at the top of the staircase taking in everything around me. The two naked still bodies glisten in the bright morning sunlight, which has returned from under cover of cloud. The three figures stand staring not quite believing what has just happened. They were still reeling from the shock of finding Josie when Mrs. Snoden's body fell from above. The blood pool widens its hold on the flat stone surrounding the body. Cloie turns deadly pale before suddenly falling over and collapsing on the ground. The stocky man and Rex quickly go to her assistance. I turn to look at the Loiselles, who are now standing by my side. They are searching for an explanation to what has just occurred. I get the feeling they wonder whether I pushed her. With the dress still clinging in my hand, I'm not exactly a picture of innocence. From their vantage point in the Peterson's apartment, it is unlikely that they saw anything until they heard the scream and saw her falling over the railing with myself in close proximity. Likewise, the three down below were occupied with Josie and, therefore, did not observe the events leading up to Mrs. Snoden's mishap. I think it wise to neglect to inform those around me of the most probable reason why Mrs. Snoden fell – because I scared the living daylights out of her– so I simply leave that part out. However, I do explain how I saw her lose her balance and begin to fall, how I made an attempt to grab her arm to stop her from doing so, and how I only got hold of her dress. It explains why it remains in my possession and, equally, why the old lady left this world in a similar fashion to how she entered into it– the only exception being the pair of pink bathroom slippers on her feet, even though one did end up in the shrubbery below. The other still remains securely on her foot– oddly, not completely out of place here in this scene of surprised misfortune: the pale white skin, the red blood, the lone pink slipper, the dead girl, the stocky man, the fainted lady, Mr. Loiselle and his speechless wife, the good neighbor Rex Targent, the old man with the dressing gown in his hand, and Philip Peterson. I didn't notice him come up behind me from out of his apartment.

"Oh my God!" he yells. "What happened here? Cloie! What are you doing to her?"

At first he didn't appear to see his daughter, Josie. The old lady's body at the foot of the staircase drew his attention. He then turned his eyes toward Cloie's figure lying still on the grass by the edge of the stone near the geranium bed. The stocky fellow was stooped over her trying to revive her and Rex was down on one knee to her side preventing Philip from seeing the entire view. Philip passes by me and the Loiselles, flies down the staircase, leaps over the old woman's body– with little more than a passing glance– and kneels down beside Cloie. For someone whom he does not love, he certainly lets on to care an awful lot. Rex Targent and the stocky fellow back away and assure him that she has only fainted. Cloie is beginning to come around. Philip holds her in his arms and tells her it is going to be alright.

Then Rex says to him, "Philip, it's Josie."

Philip Peterson turns only to see his daughter lying naked and still in the early morning sunlight. I watch his face carefully to see how he will react.

His face is without expression for a moment before finally saying, "What's wrong with her? Is she asleep?"

It takes me aback, for one thing, that he doesn't seem overly surprised or shocked his only daughter is completely nude and lying out in a public place and, for another thing, that he doesn't think it entirely impossible for her to be fast asleep while several people are standing around a dead body not more than ten yards away from where she lies. Would that not appear at least the slightest bit odd to you?

"She's not asleep," says the stocky man.

"What do you mean? What's wrong with her?" Philip Peterson is still kneeling beside Cloie holding her within a firm embrace. He has not moved towards his daughter, even yet.

"She's dead, Phil."

Still there is no expression on Philip's face.

"Cloie came down and found her about 10 minutes ago."

Cloie breaks in, "Y- Yes, it was horrible. When I came out on the terrace and saw her lying there on the lawn chair, I thought she was just sunbathing like she generally does. I was going down to tell her to get back into the apartment before somebody saw her. It's disgraceful how she lays about out here with no clothes on like that, even if it is early in the morning. I don't know why she does it. But when I talked to her, she wouldn't answer me. So I shook her and that's when she didn't move. She just lay there. And her skin was warm from the sun, but it was cold. And she wouldn't wake up. When I turned her head and saw her face, her eyes were glossy and they just stared at me. She wasn't breathing. She's dead, Phil. She's dead." Cloie is becoming upset again. "Oh Philip, it was so awful. What could have happened to her? Who could have done this to her?"

Philip is now standing over his daughter's motionless body. Shock affects different people in different ways. He seems to be staring off past her. He begins to stroke her hair, which is still a rich burgundy gloss. It shines as the sunlight touches it gently.

"We don't even know what happened to her yet," Rex adds. "Before we make assumptions and jump to conclusions, we should at least find out for certain. However, I don't quite see how a young girl like her could have just dropped dead like that. It doesn't make much sense."

The stocky man says that Phil better call the police, whereupon the Loiselles are whispering, not far from me. They are surprised no one has thought of it up until now. Rex volunteers to do so, but before leaving, he seems to pause and look at Philip as if to ask permission of some sort.

Philip nods, "Yes, of course, that would probably be a good idea, although they're not likely to be overly thrilled to find that there has been another death here yet alone two of them."

The other death to which he is referring of course has to be the poor old lady who was found lying dead in my apartment shortly before I arrived. This does not appear to be the place to stay if one is awfully fond of living. Maybe Philip Peterson is not the very best guy to know. Still, I can't really blame him for what happened to Mrs. Snoden. I am as much responsible for that as anyone. In fact, I am quite probably the one most to blame for it– if anyone. If not for me, she wouldn't be lying there right now. However, that can't be helped. What happened happened. It was an accident, pure and simple. After all, it was the old woman who was to blame for taking fright and falling. I only tried to warn her of her fate. She brought this entirely upon herself. She had used up her life and it was her time to go. I was no one to prevent that: it was not up to me. I couldn't have. No, more than that, I did not possess the ability to save her. It was not an option that lay within my hands.

Philip turns and looks back towards Mrs. Snoden's body. Up until this point in time he has not given the old woman much more than a second thought. Initially, she was what had lured him on into the viewing scene. The way she was laying there— with the blood— you could not help but take notice of her. However, she seemed to act only as a point of interest to send him towards someone a bit dearer to his heart— that being the lovely Cloie. Upon learning that she was okay, it was then brought to his attention that his daughter was in fact the one for which he should turn his concern — and so he did — in a way. It is only now that he finds the time to shed some attention on his tenant, who has been but a sideshow to compliment the main act. I suppose it is not the most meaningful way to die — in the shadow of someone else greater in importance than you. Yet it is not so sad, perhaps, as if you are to live your life the same way — as so many of us do. Now Philip seems to look upon her loss with little interest in how it came about. That much seems obvious enough.

He is more worried about how having two deaths at practically the same time is going to look to the police. It is remarkable to me how cold he seems to be towards these two, who were both unfortunate enough to die on the same day, therefore forcing them to share the attention that will naturally come along with such a detail. Granted, Mrs. Snoden might have only been a tenant and a rent cheque to him. She was old and old people tend to die. Perhaps some people just are not very good at sharing their emotions. Some people handle tragedy in different ways. Take Cloie for instance: she appears to be the overly emotional sort. Still, his only daughter has just been found dead and the only thing that he appears to show any concern about is how it is going to look to the police. Something feels very wrong here. At least the man cannot be accused of putting on an act. Maybe a little bit of a display wouldn't be such a half bad idea, though. Perhaps he has every good reason to be worried about how it is going to look.

Rex Targent goes back into his apartment to call the police. A few people– undoubtedly from the neighborhood– have gathered on the other side of the fence at the back of the garden.

There is no way to keep these unseemly occurrences from the light of day. Philip Peterson will have to deal with the police and try to explain what happened here. I will have to do a bit of explaining myself: the term witness is ingrained upon me as heavily as anyone.

Philip turns his attention away from Mrs. Snoden's body and looks soberly upon his daughter. He goes back to gently caressing her hair with his hand. After a moment of perceived thought, he startles those around him with a sudden outburst. "Why the hell doesn't someone go and get something to cover her up? We can't just leave her lying here like a piece of meat. What's wrong with you?" he yells.

I am touched to see this kind of emotion. Actually, I am relieved.

Cloie, who is still rather distraught, runs to fetch something to put over Josie.

The stocky fellow intervenes by pointing out, "Maybe that's not such a good idea. Won't the police want things left as they are?"

He does have a point.

Philip doesn't particularly agree. "What do you mean?" he snarls. "Why should they?"

Seeing his astonishment at the question, the stocky man answers tentatively, "Well, Philip, you surely realize things as they are don't look particularly good. You can't honestly think that she died of natural causes, do you? A young girl like that doesn't just drop dead all of a sudden for no apparent reason. They are going to have to look into it. You can count on that, so you can. I don't see any obvious marks on her body, but someone must have done something to her."

Cloie comes back with a blanket, which she got from Rex's apartment.

Philip takes it from her and carefully lays it over Josie's body before answering slowly, "Maybe so, but putting a blanket over her surely can't hurt too much. After all, Cloie already said that she moved her when she found her. I just don't want people staring at her anymore." He looks accusingly at the people gathered on the other side of the fence where there now stands about half a dozen curious onlookers. "Haven't you seen enough?" he shouts. "Did you have a good long look at my daughter, huh, did you?"

I myself do not feel excluded from his scrutiny, for I have a feeling the direction of his outburst is aimed at those of us who dwell inside the fence as well. There is a certain guilt that lies not far from the surface. I turn my head and look away. If he seemed indifferent at first, he is acting only as a father should now. It seems surprising how suddenly he has awakened to this new emotional standard, whereas before, the sight of his daughter lying there didn't even startle him or surprise or bring about a state of shock. It's as if, perhaps, he expected her to be that way – as if he had seen her like that before. Now does it not seem right? Does it seem sadly immoral to see her, for her to be there and somehow remain in that state of familiar shame? Is it not unholy now? Did he not know she would come to lie there in that way? Did he not expect what he must have surely seen before? Now is he not simply trying to put a stop to the turning of the cycle which comes to him constantly every time he looks upon and sees his little girl? However, now it is her time to rest. "Cover her. Turn your eyes away. We have looked enough."

Rex returns from his flat after making the call to the police. "Cover her: it won't hurt anything. Give her some dignity."

Yes. Give her some dignity.

CHAPTER 12

SOMETIMES I GET FORGETFUL

The police, along with an ambulance, arrive shortly. Rex warns everyone that the officers will likely want to question all of us so not to make ourselves unavailable. I have made up my mind that I am going to tell the police the same thing as I told the rest of them: I saw Mrs. Snoden slip and start to fall, and I tried to stop her, but by then it was too late. Even though I don't think I can actually be charged for scaring someone to their death, I'm not going to take any chances. I don't exactly know Georgian law particularly well, and I have no intention of spending what little time I have left in my life locked away in some damp fly-infested jail cell. My life at present might not be roses, but I have to admit it is still better than that, although I am not so sure you could've convinced me of that when I was on my way down here.

Everyone, including the police, seems to buy my take on what happened when the old lady fell. I consider that to be the case primarily because no one actually saw what happened from start to finish. They all saw only the finish: that much I am counting on. I alone will be punished with the guilt of knowing what really happened and I accept it to be my fair payment in turn.

The police do not know the cause of Josie's death as a fact right away. An autopsy will have to be conducted. They are treating the circumstances surrounding her death as being of a very suspicious nature and rightfully so.

Mrs. Snoden's accident seems straightforward enough in all regards. An old lady under overwhelming stress from the shock of just witnessing such an unexpected tragedy lost her balance on a staircase. You only had to wait for the inevitable, which could not help but occur. Old people tend to fall all the time. That sort of thing happens; it has to be expected. So really, there isn't anything suspicious to be found or even too seriously considered surrounding the event.

Josie's death, on the other hand, cannot be looked at without finding something suspicious in nature about every possible aspect of the entire situation. It has to be treated as suspicious, and it would surprise me or, undoubtedly, anyone involved if the police were to conduct their business along any other line of inquiry. When the police ask me if I noticed anything strange or odd earlier this morning, the night before, or even since my arrival, I do not feel it at all necessary to go into detail about what I supposedly know about the relationship between Philip and his daughter or the consistency of their past. I do not know the truth for certain, and I feel that someone a little more familiar with the family and its background should give an explanation of that nature. However, I do mention how I first saw Josie this morning. I heard Cloie's screams, and then I was the second person on the scene, apparently, directly following Cloie. I bear witness to the fact that she passed me and went down the stairs to the back garden but moments before the screaming began and only moments and seconds before I arrived on the scene myself. I don't see the need to go into detail about how I observed Josie sunbathing bareback, so to speak, the morning beforehand. That is mainly because I consider the idea in my head and I am afraid it might in some way make me appear to be a dirty old man‒ a notion that

I have no intention of letting out. Not that I am – I am not – but I can certainly see how it might look that way. I feel myself very undeserving to be seen in that sort of light now after all these years of working so desperately hard to live out a proper and right life. I also consider the idea that Rex Targent might include my name in his recollection of the events leading up to Josie's death for he, as well as I, witnessed the girl lying out here sunbathing in that way just the morning before. However, seeing as the police officer questions specifically, I make the decision that if and when I am to be later on questioned as to why I did not mention that knowledge beforehand, I will take the stance that I simply thought it to be unimportant at the time– along with an edge of the idea that, considering all in all, I am a practitioner of the older generation of moral decencies, and being so, it was only natural for me to think it not quite right to talk about seeing the poor girl in such a way. Hopefully Rex will not see fit to name me as being in possession of this information. That will be all the better. Considering the strange occurrences taking place the night before, one thing looms very large indeed. I think it far too important to fail to mention, yet I choose not to. I see myself walk the fine line between telling the police officer about how I saw the three men arguing in the middle of the night only hours before Josie's body was found and keeping this knowledge to myself. I am all but certain that no one else knows me to be aware of it. I also know it will be difficult to explain why I hid this bit of information if it comes out at a later point that I was aware of it. My decision to keep this from the police will point to me having had involvement in whatever occurred, even though there is nothing further from the truth. I know how it can and, undoubtedly, will look. Therefore, I well know that my decision to keep this knowledge secret will be irreversible. There will be no going back. And if it does turn out to be unimportant after all- or important enough, one way or the other- and one, two, or all three of the men directly involved in the midnight row see fit to bring the police to light on this turn of events, then just as well I be hidden from my past in the whole scenario. If they do not let on about this event's importance within the sequence of the whole situation- and I expect that will be the case- where do I stand then?

I was standing in the shadows when I became a part of this, and here I remain. It is a comfortable place to be- not outside but not within. It has its safety, yet it has its dangers, which cannot be overlooked. I know what I am getting myself into and at the same time I do not, but do you ever? Sometimes you are not given a choice: yours is already made. You can see on into the distance yet only so far. The rest remains waiting in search of you as much as you lay waiting for it to come to you.

I see my chance to paint these three into a corner and then watch how easily- or with what degree of difficulty- they wriggle themselves free. But I watch this opportunity pass. I hope that the depth of what happened will see its way to light and that things will play out in their own way. I have a feeling that there is more yet to transpire, and as the tides begin to flow, I want to see what further part I am to play in it all. I have little else to consider as being a form of entertainment for myself. At this stage in my life I have so little. This is something.

After I am questioned, the scene begins to clear and the bodies are moved and taken away. The police officers have finished taking statements from everyone in the building, so we are allowed to slowly drift back to our apartments to try to sort out and come to grips with all that has happened.

I return to my flat feeling quite exhausted and tired all over. It is only about 9:30 in the morning, yet it could well be evening after all that has taken place since I got out of bed this morning. Nothing particular can happen for weeks until one day something occurs that consumes the entire space surrounding it—ten days before and twenty after. It's as if those days were laid there for that one sole purpose of fulfillment for resumption. I now find myself completely emotionally and physically drained. I consider it best to return to bed. I go into my bedroom and lie down. A light nap should set me right again in no time at all. I close my eyes and feel as though there will be a very short distance for passage from this state into the next. Just as I am beginning to experience continuous continental drift, buzzing in my ears pulls at my senses. It keeps me just this side of consciousness. The humming gradually becomes clearer. It takes the form of light whispers before finally filtering down into two distinct voices. One of them sounds familiar. The voice belongs to the police officer who questioned me earlier. He appears to be talking to another officer outside my window. The screen is open just a crack, and I can make their words out clearly.

The officer who questioned me is saying how he can't be certain until the results get back from the autopsy, but he is pretty sure that the girl was smothered. There aren't a lot of marks on the body, but he noticed some light bruising around her mouth. Unless she was poisoned, he doesn't see how else she could have died. There is no other external evidence of trauma to the body, and no one is going to fool him into believing a young seemingly healthy girl would just die out of the blue for no good reason whatsoever.

The other officer is agreeing that if she was in fact murdered, they don't really have anything yet to go on to help them find out who assisted with her passing. No one surrounding her death seems to know what could have happened to the girl. He continues, "She appears to have been a bright, happy, and outgoing girl who was liked by all in the apartment complex. It is unlikely she would commit suicide. Even if she did, I don't know how she could have managed it. I suppose she could have poisoned herself or maybe taken an overdose of drugs. The autopsy should answer a lot of our questions. My bet is that she didn't do it herself. She had some help. But tell me this– what are the odds of that old lady falling to her death the same time as the girl is found dead and both of their bodies winding up as naked as sin laying out in the sunshine? You only find those sorts of numbers in Vegas on the fourth of July. I mean, those kinds of things just don't happen every second day in November."

"Now, the old lady's death is explainable. She got a shock; she lost her balance, and she fell. That's plenty straightforward enough. It's a little bit hilarious that she was the second old lady to turn up dead in this place in a little over a month whose death wasn't exactly ideal, to put it mildly. The first old lady starved to death, apparently because no one wanted to take the time to check on her. Now here's this poor old broad, left naked on the hard stone floor, neck shoved up into her torso, while that old fellow was standing up on the balcony with her dress in his hand wondering what the hell had just happened to him. According to everyone I've talked to, that's what actually happened, believe it or not. That would've been quite the sight to see. I noticed that they put a blanket over the girl to cover her up. I'm surprised they didn't do the same for the old broad. I guess they didn't think that she was important enough. I suppose they figured that she didn't have much pride left anyway. So they left her there, ass in the air‑ not exactly ideal at all, not in the slightest. Oh yes, and then there was also the case of this guy's‑ Peterson's‑ wife driving herself into the river a few years back. Geez, this guy attracts dead bodies like half‑priced caskets the day after Christmas."

"Do you think this guy Philip Peterson could have actually killed his own daughter?" the first officer asks.

"I don't know. I suppose that anything could be possible‑ that is if she was murdered, and it is our job to find out. I suppose that Philip Peterson was as capable as anyone to have done it. Offhand, I don't know why he would've wanted to kill his own daughter. However, there could've very well been a number of reasons for why he might've wanted her dead. Maybe the guy is completely out of his head. From talking with him, you would never know it, but that doesn't mean a thing. I don't know: right now I'm just guessing. It could've been one of the other tenants in the building, but by the looks of most of them, they would seem to have difficulty just getting dressed in the morning let alone commit cold-blooded murder. But anything's possible. After talking to them all, there was nothing any of them told us that would shed light on how or why the girl died. They seem oblivious to it all. If they know something, they aren't telling us. I doubt if any of them did it, though. The woman- Peterson's live-in girlfriend or whatever you want to call her- told me it was no accident finding the girl naked, and this wasn't the first time she'd lain out here in the sun without any clothes on. It seems she often did it. The woman said that the girl's father knew about it, but he didn't try to stop her- pretty free-thinking family if you ask me. It wouldn't surprise me if it was some pervert walking past early in the morning. It would've been easy enough to spot her over the back fence. Maybe he snuck up on her from behind while she was lying there and put his hand over her mouth and simply applied pressure until she stopped struggling. If he was bigger and stronger than her, in that position she couldn't have put up much of a fight. Even if there was a bit of noise, everyone in the building would've likely been fast asleep with their hearing aids turned off. They wouldn't have heard a thing."

"It didn't look as though she'd been raped, although it is hard to tell. We'll know more later on."

"Maybe he only molested her. With some guys, that's all it takes for them to get their kicks."

"We better question some of the neighbors to see if they've noticed anyone strange hanging around lately. The killer might have seen her here before and then got up the nerve to come back and have another look."

"What if it is one of the neighbours?"

"It could well be. Then again, it could very well be anyone. What if it is one of the tenants? After all, there are three men living here who have bottom floor apartments with access to the courtyard. They all would've had a very choice view of her sunbathing if they happened to look, although no one seemed to mention anything about seeing her here before. The woman was the only one who brought it up."

"What about Peterson? Did he say anything about it at all?"

"Not initially. It wasn't until his girlfriend mentioned it that he let on he knew about it, but he didn't deny it either. From the look on his face, I think that he would have preferred if she had never brought it up at all. You can see why. It is something that most fathers would deny knowing about. Still, maybe that is something we should ask the others- whether they knew about it or not. We should ask them just to see their response. It could've very well been one of those old men who got some damn strange idea in his head and then acted upon it, maybe out of some sexual inner tension. I have heard of such things."

"If they do admit to it, ask them why they didn't say anything about it before – just to see what they will say."

"So what we have here then is a stranger, a neighbour, a tenant, or Peterson himself- quite the list of possible suspects."

"That is only if she was actually murdered."

"I doubt very much if she was not."

The sounds cease. No more voices can be heard outside my window. I feel myself most fortunate to have been a silent intruder on their conversation. It puts me at a slight advantage, for I now know what to expect: I know I will in fact be questioned about Josie's nudity. What am I going to tell them? What I planned to of course if such a situation should arise. None too soon have I become satisfied in that decision, for this very moment a police officer comes a knocking on my apartment door. He apologizes for having to bother me again but quickly gets to the point of his little visit.

"Yes, yes," I answer, "I have seen the girl lying that way before- just the previous morning actually. And it's a funny thing: I just thought of it now, and I was worried I didn't tell you. I just didn't think of it when I was being questioned before. I don't know. With the whole ordeal, I must not have had my mind straight. Sometimes I get forgetful. I don't know what it is. I don't seem to be able to think as quickly as I used to. If there is too much excitement all at once, I can't seem to keep up with it. Finding out that the girl had died was overwhelming enough, and then when Mrs. Snoden fell and had her accident... well, it was all just too much to believe it could happen. I am still having some trouble dealing with it."

The officer seems convinced. He watched me intently all the while I was talking. He hoped for something more. He didn't get what he was looking for, although he hardly seems surprised. After all, what would you expect from a dotty old man of weakened mind and frail disposition? So he leaves with his duty done and his information amply collected.

As I close the door, I notice how my hand, as it rests on the door frame for support, is very dry and cracked. The other one is in the same state as the first. They remind me of an old pair of worn leather gloves I used to use for weeding the garden. I don't know how I have managed to let them get in such wretched condition. I suppose with everything that has been on my mind as of late, I have forgotten to take the time to look after myself. It has been crazy this past week. Getting ready to make the trip down here and trying to get settled into a new, strange place has really done a number on me. Just when I thought things were beginning to calm down and it looked as though I might finally find some rest, then this happens, and now I have a whole new bunch of worries. What am I talking about? I have been worrying about something or another ever since I got here. I can't remember the last time I have gone a whole day without everything seeming somehow out of place or the last time I've really had a good night's sleep. The first night I was here was the first time in over a month I'd been able to sleep through the entire night. Maybe that was what I meant. That night things were calm and quiet and I was able to find some rest. I like that feeling. I hope I will find it again. I do not like being anxious and disturbed all the time- uncertain in myself and of those around me. I don't like it at all. Then why do I seem to walk further down this path as every new day passes? Something is drawing me. No, it's more than that. Something is driving me onwards towards each approaching event. As the moments tick off the clock and the hands turn ever onward, never looking back, I find myself being pushed into the midst of every happening as it unfolds. I cannot turn away. I cannot. I can't stop it. I need this to offer- as much as it needs me to ask- every single question that is to be put before me. I have a need to know why I feel this way - why I cannot see another path to find my way back. The more I try the more I cannot understand it.

I will have to buy some Vaseline for these hands.

I feel weak. A certain kind of lingering emptiness inhabits me now. At this point in time there is nothing that appeals to me more than crawling into my bed and making a hasty retreat from reality. Sleep comes easily once I have resigned myself to it. The day's anxieties fade and disperse. The soft down-filled pillow embraces the forms of my face. I am so tired. I need this time away ... Ah, comfort and peace...

The night is clear; I can see the moonlight. There are two white pillars. They are wobbly. A pot of flowers – a horse's head is on top of one. It is near the edge. It might fall, and it's shaking. I reach in an attempt to steady the pillar before it falls. It is close – on the verge of falling over – off the edge. I can't quite reach them. I hope they stop shaking before it is too late. They are beginning to slow down. I get hold of one of the pillars, but it rolls on its edge before I can stop it.

The horse's head falls. I watch in absolute helplessness.

The rabbit lies by the side of the road. It does not move. Mrs. Loiselle smiles and laughs with the carefreeness of youth in that glorious stage of beauty in bloom. It is the finest of spring days. A warm breeze caresses my skin. The warmth invades my very bones soothing sweetly as it makes its way up the oak tree which is late in bud. It moves swiftly rustling the leaves and brushing by a squirrel as the tree bough bends above a fox and wolf side by side below. I remark to her how the sun's light glistens off her new blue frock as if it were mistaken for a piece of the sky itself. She finds me delightful. I notice how her hair is the richest of auburns, her lips are red and full, and her chest is full and inviting. She lifts her skirt. Her pantyhose are tight around her thighs. Oh, what a beautiful woman. I moan in ecstasy and squeeze her tightly. Leaving the thirst behind me, I drink in the cool lemonade savoring the sweetness and the tartness as if it were enveloped inside individual pockets of delight. I devour every last drop before setting my glass on the table to the left of the bed. I have to reach to set it there. I notice how there are *still two chunks of ice in the glass. I sink back into my bed. Her body lies soft and still beneath me. I savor the quiet comfort. I could stay this way forever.*

CHAPTER 13

HANGING OUT WITH THE STOCKY MAN

I awake from my pleasant luxury about 7:30; my rested eyes greeting a brightly lit morning. It seems to me a lovely idea to take my usual juice and have it out in the garden. The day is proving to be another warm one, and despite what happened here the day before, I am not to be persuaded away from this notion. It is too nice a morning to let go to waste. I sip my juice slowly as I imagine myself an integral part of the symphony of birdsong that prevails about me. I cannot decide which takes in a greater degree of beauty: the time I spend with my eyes closed or when I keep them open and no longer have to imagine as much. Not being able to reach a final conclusion one way or the other, I switch back and forth from one to the other at regular spaced intervals. It is as pleasant a game to play at this point in time as I can devise. I am in such a relaxed state that I hardly notice Rex Targent come out of his apartment, say good morning to me as he passes me by, and then continue on his way over to the stocky man's flat. These strangely perfect moments can come to do this sort of thing for you. Rex knocks on the door several times. He continues to knock. I am no longer quite so relaxed.

"Maybe he is away," I offer.

"There is one sure way to find out." As Rex says that, he turns the doorknob, which, in turn, reveals an unlocked door.

I wonder whether a person would be more likely not to lock their door if they were going out or if they were staying in.

"Well, what do you know," says Rex. "I think I will just let myself in and see if my ol' chum has rolled that sorry excuse he calls a carcass out of his bed yet. He was supposed to be ready twenty minutes ago: we are to go downtown." With that, he slips through the door and lets himself into the apartment.

From what I can make of the matter, Rex and the stocky fellow are fairly good friends by now. They have both lived here long enough to get to know one another, and seeing as they are about the same age and both being apparently single, it makes practical sense to expect that they should come to suit one another for casual companionship.

The sunshine is warm against my wrinkled flesh. It feels good to close my eyes and just lie back and feel the warm sensation on the lids of my eyes. I feel as though I am about to fall into sleep, even though it has only been handfuls of ticks on a clock since I arose from my past night's slumbers.

Rex exits the apartment alone. He has a peculiar look about him. If I hadn't seen him but a moment before, I would swear he looks sick. He stops just outside the door, and there he stands staring at me as if trying to relay a message to me with his eyes, apparently unable to speak.

"He's   hung   himself."

"He's hung himself? Why on earth would he go and do that? I just   cannot imagine why. He was such a nice fellow." I am starting to drift.

"He's gone and hung himself!" My eyes bolt wide open taking the rest of my entirety with them.

"What? Are   you   sure?"   I immediately realize the absurdity of my question, but by this point there is no recourse.

"Of course I'm sure." He begins to stammer uncomfortably. "I mean, I-I imagine h-he's done it himself. W-Why would anyone else do it?"

"Why would he do it?" I demand right back.

"I-I don't know. I've known him for quite a while, and there was nothing. But why does anyone do this sort of thing, I suppose?"

Why indeed? I can think of a few reasons. But by the way Rex is acting, he seems to think that he has done it himself. There has to be some reason for that.

At this time of the morning there is no one else up and about in the square. This incident, seemingly just one in a long line of unhappy events within these otherwise pleasant surroundings, has not yet attracted the attention of the building's occupants - or the outside world, for that matter. To them it still lays hidden, unseen by the warm light of day. Otherwise, only for Rex and I does it exist. We know what lays waiting behind that door. Sure enough, Philip will have to be informed and, in turn, the proper authorities will have to be brought back- if they are not already destined to pay us a visit this day. However, since the opportunity affords me now, I have this notion that I might like to see for myself why Rex seems to believe things more likely one way than the other—in regards to the trouble this morning. Quite to the opposite of Rex's opinion on the matter, you might assume it more likely that this man did not hang himself—particularly when you take into account the events surrounding Josie's untimely death. It seems only practical to believe that his death was not a suicide. So why indeed? It isn't that I really want the thrill of seeing a hanging body. Then again, who would pass up the chance? It wasn't as though I was emotionally attached to this man. I hardly knew him. We had barely spoken since my arrival. It is mainly that I want to see for myself if it looks like he did it. And maybe, as it is, I just can't pass up the chance.

Dead bodies are kind of odd to look at especially the freshly dead ones. They sort of have that misplaced feel about them, sort of like they have no place to go. They are just hanging around waiting for the next somebody coming along to decide what to do with them. When you look at them at first, it strikes you that there is very little in terms of difference between the dead ones and the live ones. It is something inconspicuous that has been removed. It is not a long ways to go from point A to destination B. You would think that there should be more difference between the two. Really, though, I suppose it is probably due to the fact that one second you are here and the next you are... Well, who really knows? The longer you look at a dead body, instead of seeing a distinct difference between the living and the still the more they tend to look alike. At times your eyes will even play tricks on you and you will swear that the dead are still breathing. But you know that that cannot be. The closeness of the two states is really quite remarkable. Mind you, the fact that the body in question is suspended from a ceiling fan with a lamp cord tightly wrapped around its purple neck with its tongue protruding out of its mouth swollen and confused tends to give off the notion that the man in question is in all likelihood no longer living– among the living, yes, but living as before, no. Of course, I am not by any length of the word an expert on the subject. In my lifetime, I have not seen any more than what I believe to be my fair share of death and dying. Everyone has their funerals to go to, and I've had mine. However, it has only been quite recently that I have enjoyed more than a healthy serving of contact with corpses. This holiday of mine seems to be bringing that out in people. There has certainly been a lot of it lately. After all, isn't there always a third, or is this the fourth or the fifth? Well, third in two days, at least. Maybe that is how it goes. I think it probably best if I do not consider this idea too much further. I am beginning to feel like I am not altogether safe myself, but if nobody else is worrying, why should I?

Sure enough, I was correct in my earlier assumption: there is indeed a breeze. The body swings just ever so slightly slowly back and forth, back and forth. The stocky man is not wearing any shoes– no socks, either. He is dressed only in a pair of worn striped pajama bottoms and a cream white sleeveless undershirt. He must have gotten up out of bed in order to hang himself. It must have been a pretty bad dream, but at least you would think that it could've waited till morning. Well, maybe it did. He doesn't look as though he has been dead that long. However, who am I to know? I think they go by how many flies have hatched on the corpse or something like that. Well, there are a couple of flies. Maybe that means he has been dead a couple of hours. Oh well, the professionals will know. They would've already done the same thing for determining the time of Josie's death, so they should've warmed to the procedure by now.

Gazing around the apartment, everything looks to be adequately in order confirming Rex's notion that suicide has indeed occurred. At first glance– as the casual observer might note– all the tell-tale signs usually associated with such an occurrence are here. The kitchen chair, which was pulled over to stand on, is tipped over lying on its side not far from the dangling figure. There is no sign of a struggle having recently occurred in the flat– nothing strewn about to indicate that. Likewise, no bruising or battery marks on the body. The cord used in the hanging was a common lamp cord. It wasn't made into a noose. It was simply wound around his neck, twice overlapped, and then firmly fastened to the central shaft of the ceiling fan. I don't see how it would've been possible for one person to hold the stocky man's bulk up that high long enough to tie the knot, even if he was subdued beforehand. I glance around the apartment as I quickly stroll its confines, but I don't notice any suicide note left as some form of explanation. Still, that isn't always the case. If you have a good enough reason to kill yourself, it seems only practical to assume that you would not want to publicize it. The lamp on the end table near the sofa appears to be the one the hanging cord was pulled from– or rather, cut from. It was clearly cut through, most probably by the pair of scissors that lie on the very same end table alongside the lamp. Rex sees them too. "He must have used those scissors to cut the cord," I say as I watch Rex.

He continues to stare at the scissors. "Yes," he mutters half under his breath.

Rex's expression causes me to wonder what he is thinking. Finally he relieves my anxiety.

"I used those scissors when I was over here yesterday afternoon." "What for?" I ask him.

"I cut a loose thread on my jacket."

"Simple enough. What's your worry?" I am beginning to sense the answer before he even speaks.

"My fingerprints will probably still be on them. What if they think that I did it?"

He turns to me. I know he expects a serious, thought-out answer for the most serious of questions, to be sure. His eyes search my facial features as he tries to read my feelings on the matter. My first instinct is simply to dismiss it with reassuring affirmation; but as it is, he does have a very good point, I have to admit. "They might, but they might also suspect us all. They would need more than that, anyhow. If you explain how your fingerprints got onto the scissors, it should satisfy them. Why else would they suspect you?" I try a light laugh for reassurance. I expect him to respond by saying "you're probably right; I've got nothing to worry about". When such a reply does not arrive in its own due time, I begin to worry. Rex seems to sense my anxiety, and for some reason, he thinks me worthy of an explanation.

"No, I didn't do it, but I know why he hung himself. I also know more about Josie's death than I let on to the police."

I hardly believe what I am hearing. To the curious, these sorts of moments almost take on an orgasmic quality. I listen with intense interest, all the while attempting to mask my own over-enjoyment.

He must know he has a willing confidant, for the depth of the story is quick to unfold. It falls on only four ears, two of which now lie dormant.

"This doesn't surprise me at all, none of it. When I look at it now, I could see it coming. I told him. I warned him about Josie. He was the fool of fools. He made the mistake of thinking she really cared. She had her own reasons. We all do, after all. Don't we? Maybe she didn't get the love she needed from her family. But it wasn't love that she was looking for here— at least, not in the normal sense of the word. She used us older gents because she could. We gave her a little of what she needed, and in return, she gave us what we were in need of. A fair exchange, I do believe. However, he didn't see it that way— the stupid old man. He believed that there was something more there. What a fool to think that he actually had a chance with something like that. Who was he kidding? Only himself, that is who. I tried to tell him. I really did. I warned him about the dangers that lay waiting when you begin down that path— convincing yourself things are a certain way when things are only that way in your own mind. You get to a certain point when there is no longer any chance for turning back. When you get to that point... well, I warned him. I'm not going to say that I didn't see it coming. Maybe I should have tried to do something more about it, but how was I to know what extremes he would go to? Realistically, there was only so much that I could have possibly done. But still, it does leave me thinking I should have done more. After Josie's death, I must admit I was a little bit scared. At that point, I just wanted to stay as far away from it as I could. I only hoped that my name wouldn't be brought into it. I really feared that it would. After all, I do have a certain involvement and responsibility in all this; there is no denying my guilt. I used Josie in much the same way as he did. Only, there was one difference with me: I knew she was using me back. Maybe she was empty inside. What she didn't get from her father she somehow got out of feeling our incredible need for her. Perhaps she needed that as much or more than we needed her. I should speak for myself, though. Obviously there were other things going on in his mind— the sick bastard. The teasing and touching wasn't enough for him. Oh God, the way she used to wind you up. She knew what she was doing; she knew just the right buttons to push. The ceiling tiles would start to sweat— it got so hot in here. She was quite the girl, she really was. One like that doesn't come along everyday. I am really going to miss her."

I sense a tear forming in the corner of his eye.

"She was much older than her years. Her childhood had made her that way, I suppose. It's too bad, it really is. She shouldn't have died. There was no need for it. If only he had played by the rules, none of this would've ever happened. But I'm not sorry for the part that I played in it. I wouldn't give it up now for the world. I loved her in my own way. But you see, I understood and was willing to accept she was only going to give me so much of her soul. The rest had been reserved for her and her alone. Something had to be. She needed that much if only for her own sanity. And I'm not saying it didn't cost me. Oh, how it has cost me and in so many ways, but you can't put a price on what we had together. On some of those nights, I imagined I had really died and gone to heaven. If I had a box where I kept only my most valued treasures in life, those nights, those very parcels of time, would, without uncertainty, hold a safe place there. But now all that is over, all due to one man wanting more than he could have. He got what he deserved. Everybody gets what is coming to them in life; you can't hide from that, you really can't."

All he has just told me set aside, I still can't help but wonder how such debauchery could have gone on right under Philip's nose without him noticing anything amiss, so I simply ask Rex. "Didn't her father know about any of this? He must have known that something was going on."

"Philip has as much blame in all this as anyone does. If he had been a better father to her in the first place, none of this should've happened at all in the last place. How hard can it be for a man to love his only child? You would think it would tear him apart from the inside out‒ knowing all this could've been avoided; that things could've been different ‒knowing all this never had to happen. That sort of thing can kill a man. If you want to know why Josie had to die, it was because one man loved her too much and the other loved her too little. If only the two obsessions had been reversed, we could all be smiling now. And I have such a nice smile too. It's really a terrible shame, such a horrible waste. Philip knew he couldn't prevent Josie from doing what Josie wanted to do. For all his faults and his shortcomings as her father, I will give him half an ounce of credit for that one. He was fully aware that if he held onto her too tightly, she was going to walk away from him for good, and he didn't want to lose another. You see, at the time, he didn't know he had already lost her. People in the center of things are seldom aware of such things. That's the sad part of it- not that there is ever really a happy part. Some of us appear destined to lose everything we hold dear in life. Perhaps Philip had come to realize that and that could've been why he seemed to try so hard to push Josie away. He was only trying to prevent her from getting too close to his heart. He knew the dangers that lay in wait for her there. However, destiny has a certain way of finding those who belong to it. If not for that, none of us would be here now. Oh yes, we are all here now and that is something you can count on. Once Philip had resigned himself to the idea that things were out of his control, it was far too easy for him to stand back and watch as the pieces fell into place. He knew what was going on, but he couldn't stop it if he wanted to."

"One night Josie came to my apartment. I know he followed her there. He was standing all by himself outside the window. I knew he was there, and at first

I...I really half expected him to come charging in and bash the hell out of me, but he didn't. He just stood outside and watched. He watched as Josie enticed me with her soft looks and tender words. He watched as she removed her top then lifted her tartan skirt and slowly peeled off her nylons. When she opened up my pants and pissed all over me, there he was standing outside watching all along. From that point onward, he was part of it. I wasn't worried anymore; I didn't care what he did. Maybe I even kind of hoped he would try and do something about it if only for the sake of Josie herself. What could he do to me? After all, it was his daughter who had seduced me. And he had watched the whole thing. He was part of it then. He'd had his chance to do something right there when it happened, but all he had done was cry. I thought it was raining that night. I think that I cried too. And Josie, well, she had been crying for years. I kind of feel sorry for Philip, but one sad soul deserves another, I'm to guess. I have a feeling he knew what was going on before that. I think he needed to see it in actual colour, though, that's all. After that, well, we all sort of had a quiet understanding. Philip wasn't going to be a father to that girl. I figured that I was more of a father to her, and that's what she needed from me more than anything. No matter how twisted our relationship was, at least I was able to give her something in that regard. He on the other hand– he who hangs there now... He jabs at the body allowing it an open invitation to swing. "All that he ever tried to do was take, take, and take." Rex's voice rises in anger.

I can sense the hatred he holds for this man. He jabs the body some more– each time causing me to fear it will come crashing down, bringing us some very unwanted attention to be sure.

"In reality, this man was no friend to Josie. He took then, and he has taken now. He wanted only what he needed; he never thought about what she was in need of. He thought she loved him. He couldn't believe that she would ever use him. How could she do that to him? How could she not? We are all in need of love. However, we accept what we can and what we cannot have. How could he possibly think that someone such as she could ever love him in that way? How foolish could the man have been? He used her in much the same way as I did, but he only wanted to possess her. I took care of her. Somebody had to.

I knew she was going to stop seeing him. She was getting tired of the way he was treating her. He had become too controlling. She told me he had even hit her on a few occasions. He had become very jealous; he wanted her all for himself. And I could see his distaste growing towards me as well. I should have known something like this was going to happen. It was bound to. He could not stand the idea that she would play him for a fool– the fool he really was. Two wives had already left him, and his family had practically abandoned him."

I know a little about how that feels.

"And all for the very same reason; nobody could love him. But that only made him in need of it all the more. He just couldn't understand why someone he wanted so badly would not want him back. He could not accept the notion that he had nothing she wanted– only his money. And that being only enough to amuse her for a time, she was now through with him. So he is now through with her. Now I say it should've never happened, but with everything the way it was, I don't really think it could've turned out any other way."

It is quite the story. It seems to make perfect sense– how all this could have come about. It started with a troubled girl- the product of a troubled father- and the loneliness of old age. Put together, two souls somehow found solace in fantasy until the fantasy became no longer enough, and then the beautiful dream turned into a nightmare. I can well see it happening. I can also see how easily I myself might've played a part in this; perhaps, if circumstances were a little bit different. It is true but sad to think nonetheless. There is something I can't help but keep wondering though. It hangs there, not unlike being on the verge of a dense fog, clouding over what now should be the clearest of views. The night leading up to the morning they found Josie I awoke out of my sleep to find it still night. I remember it as if it was but a dream, yet I know it was not. The darkness remained intact within the edges of twilight. The mood had been set so that I could not help but remember afterwards, and I am certain of what my eyes saw – well, I was certain then, not as sure now. But I know what I saw: the three men together. Then Josie turned up dead. I am almost afraid to confront Rex with this. He might try to convince me I was only dreaming, but the way I figure it he can do only one of two things: either confirm or deny it. If he confirms it, then I will know what I saw was real. If he denies it, I will be no worse at a loss than I am at present. I decide I should at least give him a chance to try and clear things up for me. The rest of his story fits. Maybe he has an explanation for this as well.

I can choose to stay silent now and wait to tell the police what I thought I saw. However, seeing Rex's predicament, with the level and conditions of his involvement and the clear difficulty of the circumstances at hand, I feel I sort of owe it to him to let him know beforehand what I saw on the night in question. Perhaps it is partly that I can too easily see myself standing where he stands now. And knowing that well, I would surely wish for the same opportunity to be afforded me.

Loneliness can sometimes cause a man to follow unstraightened paths, and you don't always realize the full extent of the choices you make in life until it has become all too late. By then, you are enveloped inside the deep end of a situation, not quite knowing how you got there. You are gasping for air in the worst of ways, and you pray desperately for someone– anyone– to throw you a lifeline to cling to. It is not that hard to imagine, not when I am heading towards the closeness to such a point in my own life. So I make up my mind. I will throw him his lifeline and see where it falls.

"I saw the three of you that night— you, Philip, and him. I saw you all through my window the night before Josie was found."

There, it is done. Now all that remains to do is sit back and await his response. As I watch the colour slowly drain from his face and follow his eyes in their decline toward the floor tiles, where they come to rest, it occurs to me that perhaps Rex Targent was more involved in Josie's death than he is letting on and perhaps so was her father, Philip.

"I know this looks bad, and I can honestly tell you it is. I didn't think anyone saw us that night. Through your eyes, I know how it looks. I can't say that I didn't have anything to do with her death because we both know I did, but I didn't kill her and neither did Philip. This sad excuse right here did it, as I've already told you. He did it, and then he didn't know what he was going to do. He actually came to me for help, and I was fool enough to help him. Josie went to his apartment that night to break it off with him— just like she told me she would- and he couldn't handle it. He said he snapped. He felt so much rage that he had no idea what he was doing. He told me he felt so awful that he wanted to put a bullet through his head. Where is a gun when you need it? It made me feel sick. I knew it was going to happen, yet I didn't do a damn thing to stop it. I felt like putting a bullet through his head right there. I didn't help him because I felt sorry for him: I knew that if he was arrested for her murder, it would all come out and my name would be dragged into the whole stinking mess too. I sure the hell don't need that, especially not at this point in my life. That's not the way you want to be remembered. The possibility of me going to jail doesn't seem altogether too appealing either.

Maybe what I've done isn't right- in the full extent of the word- but I've done it out of my own need and out of love for her. I needed her, and she needed me. I'm not going to pretend to be ashamed for that. I'm only sorry it had to end the way it did. And I'm ashamed that I didn't wring the bastard's neck myself." Rex Targent's face began to smile. "Philip wanted to, you know. You are right about what you saw: Philip was there that night as well. I had to convince this piece of work here that it was better to include ol' Phil in this than to have him all by himself on the outside of the situation looking in. Keep your enemies closest of all, don't you know. Philip has long past been in it way too deeply for him to claim innocence now. He no more than I would want anything of this nature to come out from under the Georgian pine shadows. He will stay silent. I know that. He would have as much- or more- to lose as anyone."

Rex's smile is once more intended for me.

"Even you, my friend, are not without guilt, and I have a feeling that you know it only too well. It's funny: you probably didn't even notice it while it was happening, but one thing led you to another, and before you were to know it, you yourself had become involved. See how easy it was? There was nothing to it. It was a piece of cake. Now isn't it sweet?"

I not only know it; I understand it all too well.

"I suppose you know that that is the reason why I'm telling you all this. You are as likely to talk as our good friend- Mr.-I-can't-find-any love-so-I'm-just-hanging-around-over-there." His laughter suddenly becomes more serious. "Am I not right? You're now in this too. Aren't you?"

I was dragged into all this without my knowing— as before me, I am now sure Philip Peterson was. When he began his descent, he probably never figured on there being no exit signs. As he continues on his way down the hall, seeing the light growing dimmer and dimmer, he probably doesn't even recognize the spot where he stands right now. I hardly recognize it myself. Rex wonders where he stands also. The dead man wonders no more: he knows where he stands.

I can tell the police what I now know and face up to my own guilt in all this. After all, in reality, the part that I play in this is but a small one. I am only the outsider on the very edge of it all. Yes, I myself am guilty of involvement. I watched, but I did not know what I was seeing. At the time, moths looked like butterflies. At the time, perhaps Philip, or Rex, or anyone did not know what they were seeing, either. At any time they saw only one event before knowing that it would always lead into another. Can it be that they are no guiltier than I am? Were they to know things would turn out this way?

Everything becomes blurred; I find it hard to think clearly. I find myself so easily tired these days. It would be for the best if all this would just go away. If we could go back and simply not begin down our paths towards this central event, it could disappear as if it never happened.

Sometimes one man alone does something and no one knows. It is hard to know what is on a man's mind. It is best to keep quiet where all are concerned sometimes. Silence is golden, and silence makes it all go away. I will keep quiet. I never saw a thing. I can see the relief on Rex's face. It is the result that he hoped for.

"Good man, I knew I could count on you. You know what is for the best. You are right in your judgment: it has to be this way. You are right in what you are doing and I want you to know that. I may be a lot of things in all this, but I'm no murderer. I didn't do it, and I don't think that Philip did it, either. When I told him what had happened, he wanted to kill him. I really believe he did. It was all I could do to restrain him. It was not easy: I felt like doing it myself, but as I've said before, I'm no killer. I thought that the best way to go about it was to try and convince Philip it had been an accident, and that he had never intended to kill her. The truth is that he never even thought to pretend there was anything accidental about the way Josie had died. He was never that clever. However, with the way things presented themselves to me at the time, I believed it to be the only steadfast option available in persuading Philip not to wring a second neck in the same night. Once Philip had convinced himself this man's murder was in no way going to be a plausible solution to the set of problems we now saw before us, if it had ever been thought possible, he withdrew into himself even further. He closed out what little feeling he had left. It was like turning a valve closed and proceeding to watch as the final droplets of water fell away toward the floor. After this collapse, there was nothing more to come, no more tears to fall. He was emotionally drained. He had grown colder in an instant. He had been withdrawn in a lot of ways before that, but even so, it was as if he had stepped from day to night. After that he was like a man on a mission. He took control of the situation firmly. He treated the man who, with such severe permanence, had extinguished the life of his only daughter as if he were simply another routine problem. I watched his eyes. He stared right through him like he wasn't even there. Everyone has a way of coping with ordeal that suits only them, and Philip chose to escape in his. It was his suggestion to bring her body out into the courtyard and lay it on the sunning chair. He knew how she liked to go out there on early mornings to enhance the view. As I've told you before, he knew everything that tended to go on around this place. Philip Peterson was right in the middle of it. He said it would've been like any other familiar morning. She would've gotten up to go out and sun herself until someone admiring the delicate scenery came to realize that the object of their attention— the scenery— had become far too still. You can imagine how it might have happened. The way he saw it some dysfunctional degenerate passerby got hold of an eyeful and simply couldn't help themselves. You know how it is with those sorts; you can never tell when something like that might happen. It is anyone's good guess who may be the next victim of that sort of thing. There is just no safety to be found these days; you can be well sure of that, so you can."

"I wonder who could have done it. It is no matter. Those sorts all tend to be pretty much the same. And they are sure to be found just about anywhere lurking in the shadows waiting for the next opportunity to come idling their way. Not rushing their way by any means: the troubled tendencies always occur by means of idling. They are funny that way, so they are. And you do know who 'they' are, don't you? You know, the ones who always come an idling. It's sad to think how frequently that sort of thing happens these days. It can occur anywhere and in any place, even in your own backyard-especially in your own backyard.

"Philip knew what he was talking about, and I had to agree. That was easy enough to do. Wasn't it? Was it not? After all, it was for the best. And what was for the best, unquestionably, without even trying or attempting to deny it, was to distance ourselves from that girl's death, no matter how tragic a notion it seemed to be at the time. Not a single one of us wanted our involvement to be known. We were long since past redemption. We had crossed over the point of innocence on that matter. We had little choice but to follow this road for the full distance of the mile. There was to be no turning back. Want it or not, we were now in this together. We had our own choices to make, and we all chose this. And now it is your time to choose. You're half way there already; traveling the rest of the way is simpler than you could possibly imagine. You may not even know it, but you are very close to being there. Just forget that it ever happened, and it will all go away. It will all go away, all in a sweet restful dream as you sleep on the sugar from the boughs of the pines, as words of your lover fall from your mind, and you could never be happier as you turn back the time. Just forget. You don't want them to find out about you. They don't need to know. It will be our little secret. It will all be forgotten, and no one needs to know. We will all be safe; you will be safe. I trust that you now know that too?"

I don't care who did it. What does it matter anymore? Rex is probably right about him hanging himself. The stocky man could no longer accept what he had done; he couldn't live with himself. He couldn't stand the idea of what might happen if he was to be found out, and he feared he would be found out. Maybe this was an easier path for him. He couldn't live with the path that they had chosen for him, so he chose his own. It all seems to make sense- everything I was told. It will be easier this way. He created a loophole for us to escape; we owe him due thanks for that. We found ourselves abreast upon a cliff of perilous heights, and some of us treaded too close to the edge. This man stepped too far, and he had to be the one to fall. The rest of us have been given a second chance to make our way back to safer ground. This is a chance for us all. Why not take it? What is there to be gained any other way? Everything lost has already been lost. There is no purpose in putting anything more up for the losing. Enough has been lost already. Now the best thing to do is only to forget. I will be quiet. I never saw a thing.

"You had best do something about those scissors then." Rex smiles a gracious smile. He now knows I am on side. His eyes come to rest on the slim, silver-sided, pale blue-handled, twin daggers that lie silent on the end table top back dropped by the smooth varnish finish and the severed cordless lamp. "I'm not sure if the police will buy your story about borrowing them. They might believe you. Even if they do, it can't help but bring unneeded attention your way. They have to explore all possible leads. It will probably be better if they find your fingerprints to be noticeably absent."

Rex looks worried. "Does the lamp cord look like it could've been yanked out causing it to break?"

I don't think so. "It looks as though it's been cut- no way getting around that. If you take a pair of pliers and pull the remaining piece of cord out of the lamp base, that might work. But even then, the other part of the cord, which he hung himself with, might still look like it's been cut. I don't know. It might be hard to tell. But I think that the police are pretty detailed about these things."

"What if I just wipe my prints from the scissors?"

"No, that wouldn't work, and then it would really look like it was murder. Where would his prints have miraculously vanished then?"

"That's right", Rex agrees. "I can't do that. I'm glad that I have you on side. You certainly have a mind for this. Are you sure you haven't done this sort of thing before? Ha!" Rex has a special way of making you feel at ease, even under the most trying of circumstances.

"I wouldn't be doing this sort of thing now if it weren't for the sake of a certain Mr. Rex Targent. And the fact remains; when you find yourself in such an unsavory situation as this, you are forced into reasoning your way out of it by using the best of your abilities– whatever those abilities tend to be. And if I happen to be at all good at it, it is through no fault of my own. I can assure you of that, sir." I laugh.

"I would like to get rid of those scissors. We could replace that pair with another set. He might even have another pair here in the apartment."

I hope that is so because I don't think that I have a pair in my possession, and I guess that Rex is lacking in cutters himself if he has to borrow this fellow's. I don't know where we will find a pair otherwise. I hate to think the nearest store. And it certainly won't do any good going door to door knocking on all the neighbor's houses. That could possibly draw undue attention to us, even if it is only in the smallest of ways– to be in such a desperate need of scissors at this time, out of all times such as this. "Even if we do find another pair, how will we get his fingerprints onto the new ones?"

"Now here you are onto something. The same way we would've gotten them onto the old ones, of course. Of course! Why didn't we think of that before?"

"You mean me, I assume?"

"Yes, you're quite right, indeed, my good man: Me is correct. Why didn't I think of that before?"

"Why thank you, I think." I have a feeling that Rex's thought is about to blossom.

"We simply wipe the old scissors clean of all prints and then carefully, with intense delicacy, install the establishment of entirely new ones. Is that not a beautiful notion if ever there was one?" Rex is now caught up completely.

"It could well work but only if we're to do it right. We'll have to be careful."

"Precisely, we can have it no other way."

"His hands have already started to stiffen. That could be a problem. We have to make it look as though he actually gripped the handles in order to cut the cord. It will not do to just have a print here and another there; it has got to look real."

Rex goes into another room leaving me momentarily alone. The swinging corpse stands in as company for my thoughts. As the stocky man's body stirs uneasily back and forth in the early morning breeze, I really start to wonder what I have gotten myself into. I am beginning to think it might make more sense for me to simply turn right around and walk out the door and go back to my apartment before I get myself even deeper into the middle of this whole thing. However, my thoughts quickly become redirected, for Rex emerges from the other room with a pair of brown leather gloves. He proceeds to take a handkerchief out of the palm of one hand and wipe the scissors clean of all possible telling marks. He then brings me straight back into the depth of this rather unseemly plot leaving my former ideas well behind me on the shelf to gather dust, not unlike a pair of this man's well worn shoes left behind him now to accumulate powder in the back reaches of some old closet. He hands me one of the gloves. My job is to steady the dead man's arm while Rex, with such extreme delicacy, applies the appropriate prints to the scissor handles. With that completed, the scissors are returned to their proper placement on the end table- by the severed lamp; Rex returns the gloves and the hanky to the other room; and I am left to thoughtfully admire the way he, with such a pleasant degree of supreme technical merit, touched each of the man's fingers to the surface of the scissor handles. He took such care to ensure that just the right area of print was on the suitable part of the surface- gripping the scissors with his own gloved hand first and then copying that out exactly in the repetitive form of doing one finger at a time, not resting until this precisioned masterpiece was at completion.

Rex comes back into the room, and we quickly but thoroughly give the place a sound once over to ensure that there is nothing that might suggest it was not a suicide, which, of course, will only naturally be assumed. We make certain that there is no further sign of anything that might draw even a trace of unneeded attention towards any of us- other than the dead man, of course. We then make absolutely sure that no one is stirring out in the courtyard. Finally we check all the facing windows and doorways that could present the possibility of viewing our exit.

Feeling suitably safe, I swiftly make my leave of the apartment and return once more to my sunning chair in the courtyard where I continue my morning nap.

Shortly thereafter I am disturbed by a noise, which sounds like footsteps close by. I open my eyes only to observe Rex Targent, a neighbor of mine from across the ways, walk out of the stocky man's apartment with the most troubled of expressions upon his face. I would swear he has just seen a ghost- or the possibility of one's apparition. I ask him, "What's the matter? Is everything alright?" There is an uncertain stretch, which lasts many lengthy seconds in time, where he can only stare blankly- completely understandable in this situation under these circumstances. At last he manages to speak. He explains how only moments before he went looking for his neighbor who was supposed to meet up with him in front of the building to go into town with him. When he didn't show up within a reasonable allotment of time, he figured he had slept in- entirely reasonable given the hour of the morning. And while he was in the process of attempting to rouse that fellow from his slumbers, finding the door to his apartment unlocked, he entered only to discover with the greatest of horror his casual friend and neighbor hanging from the ceiling fan cold as dead could be.

I am suddenly taken aback myself— not complete shock but by a degree deemed appropriate for the situation. However, it soon becomes clear to me what must be in need of doing. I, without further waste of the day, escort Mr. Targent up to Philip Peterson's flat, and in spite of our present state of unsettlement, we do our best to explain.

Philip Peterson seems just as upset as we are. It surely comes as an incredible shock to him, especially considering all that has recently happened. He shows to be a strong man, though— of a quality test of character. He demonstrates a level mind and a solid handle on the situation. He goes ahead and phones the police, once again stating to them that he will be requiring the need of their services.

Cloie, having just awakened out of her sleep, overhears Philip telling the police a man hung himself. Cloie screams. That is quite disturbing. I hope that no one saw us enter into the stocky man's apartment earlier this morning. It seems unlikely that anyone did at that hour of the morning. Everyone was still asleep in bed– anyone who might've had a view of the courtyard and, therefore, a view into the nature of our activities. I doubt if there is an early riser in the bunch other than Rex Targent and myself. Even if Philip Peterson belongs in that selectively grouped category– even if he is an early bird– Philip Peterson would be wise to keep his mouth shut. I figure that he will want to stay silent, so all should be quiet. There is really little need to be disturbed.

The next couple of weeks pretty much go along as might be expected. It doesn't have to be said that, for the police, visiting Peterson's condominium is becoming too much of a habit, and habits that are forming can be known to resemble a little more than might be excused with coincidence alone. There is only so much that our good friends on the police force can do about it, in spite of what they want to believe. The real proof– and in the end, what they really have to rely on– is always to be left up to the cold hard facts and, therefore, the evidence. The fact remains that the evidence points to one individual– one man. His own sickness caused the downfall of the otherwise innocent people who surrounded him. Some were only affected indirectly, others directly and others even more so, but to each he brought about so much pain and suffering. The three deaths that occurred over the last couple of days can all be blamed on his— this man's— means of corruption; although, the old lady's passing was only a mere spin-off from the primary damage he inflicted. She held a certain level of responsibility for the cause and effect of her own death. It is almost a certainty that the elderly woman who occupied my apartment before me was entirely safe from such corruption; it would be quite difficult to make the stocky fellow the scapegoat for that whole escapade. It is unlikely that he had anything to do with it. The worst thing you can possibly blame her death on is a form of neglect. It has never in any way been proven that a crime was committed. At most, it was only the crime of guilt and that guilt belongs considerably to Philip Peterson. But now that he has come to have so much of it these days— and in so many ways— it has grown rather difficult to fault him too terribly much for that past set of circumstances. You can almost understand it. Sometimes you expect things to be a certain way; you aren't looking for things to be difficult. You don't always notice at first when they are. It is only afterwards you wonder how you could've possibly missed all the obvious signs. However, keeping all that aside for the moment, the lone disturbed dead man most certainly held responsibility where these other deaths are concerned. Due to the way things have turned out and due to all the evidence found to exist, you can't help but believe that the one and only man who could've been held accountable for those unfortunate events was he and he alone. That is not so hard to believe. After all, everything does appear to make perfectly good sense. Regardless of anything else, we can only go with what we have, and what we have here is an apparent suicide brought on by a man's committal of murder, which was brought about by his own inability to accept reality. That reality, of course, involved a girl less than one third of his age no longer being in love with him- if she ever was.

Nobody else is admitting knowledge about any of it. No one saw anything unusual, and no one is aware of anything out of the ordinary going on. So in all reality of the situation, what more are the police to do but close the book on this case and forever after come to refer to it as a simple- or, perhaps, not so simple- murder suicide? It is hard to say what it is, but what else could it be? That seems to make the most sense. Anything else would be much more difficult to explain - much harder to imagine. So it is quite fortunate to have all things leading to that one and only possible outcome. It has really worked out for the best- for almost all who are concerned. There will, of course, be further police inquiries. There has to be: it is only to be considered an act of routine business.

As it was expected, the stocky man's death is deemed a suicide- not to be confused with one of convenience, but perhaps it had a lot to do with that as well. The man didn't leave a note to explain his suicidal notions; although, that is not completely out of the ordinary all considering. And considering it all, there is little choice but to rule that the very same man who chose to take his own life also took the life of the poor young girl.

Details concerning how Josie was brought to her death are slow to emerge over the next couple of weeks. It was by strangulation. He choked her until she could breathe no more- until the last, final gasp of breath was squeezed from her tender young throat.

Josie was young- only fifteen; however, she did engage in sexual intercourse. The tests carried out by the medical examiner confirmed that to be the case. Interestingly enough, it didn't take place in the recent past making it practically impossible to determine who had sexual relations with her. Those results cannot provide definitive proof that the stocky man was involved with her in that fashion; however, there has never been any need for them to do so. His motive for murder was primarily love, not necessarily sex. In all likelihood, his relationship with Josie Peterson was of a physical nature, but whether that is true or not, it has no bearing on the outcome of the findings one way or the other. Now with that said, if it does come to be proven that someone else had such a relationship with the late Miss Peterson, well, then you can certainly see how that might be considered a whole other case entirely. Of course, nobody did for nothing can be proven either way. It is most probably for the best: it keeps things simpler.

I get a lot more sleep over the next short while. The police wrap up their investigation into the deaths in the building, and the inquiries draw to a close. When questioned, nobody knows anything that tends to differ from what everyone already suspects. Nothing is found to dilute the strong suspicion that the stocky man committed a murder suicide. Perhaps they weren't done directly together; however, the decision for suicide followed closely after. So, therefore, with the strong evidence intact on all fronts, the case is deemed closed.

CHAPTER 14

A TIME FOR AIRING OUT

Now that things have settled down, it is quiet and I like that. You can hear yourself think when the warm southern breeze flutters by your ear. You can make out what it is trying to say to you when it rustles gently through your hair; you know its words are of a friendly nature. I begin to accept time on its terms. Once you realize you have been given only a set amount of living in this life and grow to understand that it has all been decided for you, it then becomes easy to enjoy your time for what it is. By that point it is usually too late for most. I am fortunate to have been delivered this freedom before the hour is quite nine tenths past. Any more, and then it would be too late for me as well- not unlike the many others it turned out to be too late for. It is funny how I get this chance.

The Loiselles are haunted by their disturbing, troubling memories and decide to move away from the building. There are plenty of places in this country that will make them feel at home. The Loiselles have a way of blending into the framework. They do it so well that it could easily work against them– so well, in fact, that it might be hard to miss them when they are gone. Enough of such talk. At my age, I don't like to think about that sort of thing.

Rex Targent continues to be a good neighbor to me. He keeps to his own business and, in turn, lets me take care of mine. When, on occasion, our interests do happen to cross paths, he is always quite willing to lend a helping hand. In all actual truth, a man better in use one would be hard pressed to find. We continue to get together for the odd drink and talk. We remain on friendly terms, but I mostly keep to myself. I spend a lot of time alone, which suits me just fine. By now, I have grown rather accustomed to it.

Philip Peterson hasn't changed very much since his daughter's death. He does a good job of keeping his appearance together for the sake of those left around him. He hardly misses a step as he conducts his everyday business around the building. If you did not know about the recent goings on here, it would be most difficult to imagine what has just taken place or the extent of the division the man has gone through. From the time of Josie's passing until the point the stocky man took his own life, there was definitely a difference to be noticed in Philip Peterson. If it was ever thought possible of the man, it was then that he showed distinct signs of actually coming apart at the seams. It seems to have passed though with the man's hanging.

Cloie has kept up a sufficient grieving campaign for quite a while after Josie's death- much longer a period than anyone could've really expected or asked of her. The tears seem to come all too easily; so often she suddenly thinks of her, and then how the tears rain down. And so frequently it does rain; I sometimes can't help but think it too much. No one expected her to care so deeply and in such a passionate way for the girl; although, I myself have never thought her to be a bad actor. But who am I to guess? After all, that is what we are doing here- guessing, expecting things. For all I know, Cloie cares deeply for the people who surround her and, perhaps, has suffered a very real and profound loss with the girl's passing. How is anyone to know? The day before, upon seeing me, the lady actually cried on my shoulder. I hardly knew what to do; it made me feel rather uncomfortable. I think it will be best to avoid her as much as possible after that.

Now that the old building has aired itself out, it is once again time for new people to take up residence in the roomy yet empty apartments surrounding the pleasant garden courtyard. An elderly little man has already moved into the apartment that used to belong to the poor old dear who lost her balance and collapsed off the balcony on the morning they found Josie Peterson. He took up residence shortly after it was rendered vacant. There was hardly any time at all between the old lady's death and the new tenant's arrival. It came about so briskly that it seemed like only hours of separation; although, it was actually days but few of them at that. If she had died on a Friday, the little old man would've been settled in by the ensuing Wednesday—hardly any time at all.

The stocky man's flat takes a while longer to forget what it saw and whose it was. It will be hard to evict the lingering atmosphere from that place. There are bits and pieces of him left: fragments of time and shadows; stencils of his personality, which have stayed behind due to his parting being far too sudden and abrupt. However, most of those will fade in time as a new personality settles in, but some will linger on – always.

CHAPTER 15

SOUTHERN BRUNETTES

Margaret Kenton is an elegant southern brunette. She is slim but shapely in her own way, and she prefers dressy pleated skirts and to wear her hair at shoulder length. Her locks are held up in the back by a sterling silver barrette formed in the shape of a swordfish. She wears a kind smile and possesses the soft sweetly caressing voice to match. The first time our eyes meet her warm smile gives me comfort inside. It seems silly at my age, but she sort of makes me blush. I felt it the moment I laid eyes on her. I knew I could like her very much. My initial impression will prove more truthful with time: we are to become the best of friends.

Margaret moves in across the courtyard from me on a Thursday morning, four weeks and a day after the apartment suddenly became empty. It is a very nice apartment: all the flats surrounding the garden are ideally located with the most splendid of views. She was really quite fortunate to secure an apartment in a building like this. Someone must've been smiling down on her from above: she has been put amidst the wonderful scenery and set on a quiet southern street in this pleasant Georgian town. She has to wonder how she found fortune enough to get accepted into such a place. I can see how she might be curious as to why the old occupier is no longer hanging around: everything about the building and apartment seems to be so very nice. "Nice and tidy" is how she words it the first time we speak on a casual basis. That is how she finds the place. I'm not quite certain what she means by that. Does she mean the building or the surrounding town? Maybe it is just her apartment. However, she would be right on all counts regardless of any specific intentions she might have.

Our first conversation is not a long walk in the woods. It is early morning in the courtyard garden− the place where all things tend to transpire about their troublesome ways. It holds a certain degree of lesser importance that those seeds of trouble bare out their origins elsewhere. The sun is fully shining when chance finds me in the garden outside her apartment door. Here I stroll admiring the tiger lilies and lustrous orchids decorating the beds along the courtyard wall. Following this path of beauty leads me straight to her door, which just happens to find its way open. Having no proper place to hide or a sufficient amount of time to run, I brace myself for the meeting. I am not prepared for making her acquaintance. I want so much to make a good first impression. Being tongue-tied and not quite able to explain why she finds me standing alone outside her door on such a morning as this isn't exactly what I have in mind. Although she might not find it all the way surprising for that to happen, being old and mindless is not the light that I desire to be lit with, especially in her eyes. So, being without a suitable alternative plan at my immediate disposal, this is to become our first chance meeting in the garden.

She likes my warm eyes: they have a certain crinkling way about them. When I rest my gaze upon her, my facial expressions communicate my feelings more than the words I speak. I am old and life weary. My heart has been ground downward over the years, but in spirit I am still quite young. She doesn't know why, but she feels more at home in my company than anywhere else in recent times. Maybe in some way I remind her of her father-bless his soul. Her dad passed away a few years ago. It seems like longer. It has been a while since she's heard his voice. She misses talking to him, but she misses a lot of other things too. I make her feel the same warm way her father used to and she needs that. Two failed marriages behind her, she is forty-six and trying once again to start all over. For a while there, she really believed she would make it on her own, be independent, find happiness by herself. Well, congratulations are in order: she has found herself, sure enough, but she also finds she is lonely- as lonely as she can ever remember feeling. There isn't much left of her family; back home little closeness remains for her now. Friends and acquaintances have all just come and gone throughout her entire life, and where they tend to go is only for the next one to know.

She decides the thing for her is going to be another fresh start. She has taken the time to look inside herself, and she has seen what she needs. She has found that out, and now she is set on getting out there and acquiring it. She isn't in any kind of mood for making apologies for what she wants either. What she wants out of life now is to have company of an enjoyable kind, not the kind she had the distinct pleasure of having before– twice wise, to make matters doubly worse. She spent eleven long years with her first husband. No matter how hard or long she might try, she will never have that time back. It is gone for good. That train has already left the tracks. It is headed over the cliff of no return with her eleven years riding smack dab in the middle of the damn caboose. She withstood eleven years of watching him drink his life– and hers– into the ground, and all the while she lived along the backside, baby, of the stinking American dream. She got herself out of that rut only to stumble on into a perfectly nice fellow of a different sort less than seventeen months down the line. He worked hard at shaping her into what he hoped would be an exact replica of his mother– without a whole lot of cooperation from herself, she wants to add. She might laugh now, but surprisingly enough, she put up with it for nearly seven and a half years before she finally buried his mother. In doing so, it gave her a grand idea, and she buried him too. This time she is going to be smart about it, as she should've been all along. This time she is in it for money– for comfort of character as well as for means.

She wants the kind of companion who feels himself most fortunate to be with her and, in turn, will be quite willing to reward her handsomely. A generous older man can be the most absolute of godsends for a middle-aged woman. Yes, when she came here, she knew exactly what she was wanting, and as things are turning out, it looks as though she will be getting what she needs as well.

We meet on a few more occasions over the course of the next couple of weeks. As time progresses, it isn't long before Margaret Kenton and I become very good friends. She wears a lot of skirts. She seems to prefer neutral coloured ones with pleats. They suit her well: she has very nice legs. And I'm sure she knows that, for I can think of no better reason for why she shows so much of them off so much of the time. I don't mind admiring them; looking at them relaxes me. We both seem to sincerely enjoy the other's company. We do a lot of talking about a lot of things. So many long Georgian afternoons find themselves filled by Margy and I talking away the hours day after day. We talk about a lot of things— things we haven't talked to anyone about in a long time. She tells me I have a certain way of making her feel comfortable. I have to admit that I can't help but feel the same way when I am enjoying her company. She tells me about how as a little girl she used to play house with her porcelain dolls. She would pretend that she was all grown up and dream of the happy home and loving relationship she hoped to have one day in the future. She describes the colors and patterns of her dolls' dresses. Mary Anne, her favorite, wore her long silky hair in locks of dark richly textured burgundy and her fine little dress had the straightest of pleats in the skirt. She made certain of that herself by spending many long hours delicately folding them, each into their own special place. She isn't sure what happened to that doll. Perhaps she too has grown up and realizes that life doesn't always hold dreams of sunshine in the cards for you. A doll cannot play pretend forever, and that is now such a long time ago.

I never thought that I would meet someone like Margy again. After my wife died, I really believed that that would be it for me: by this point in my life all the romance would be over. I thought I had finally figured it all out. I would no longer need anyone‒ or much of anything‒ anymore, and certainly no one would ever need me. I thought I had already made up my mind about that. Yet, here I am now counting on her being near me and not wanting her to go away. When she is with me, I feel at home‒ more than I can remember feeling in the longest of times. I want to feel that way again‒ everyday. I really need her now, and I am beginning to realize the sheer severity of my longing. As I watch, it is like sleeping; it gradually overtakes me in the night of my life.

I haven't received word from my daughter or my little angel Sandra in quite a while. It has been a long time since I have last heard her soft sweet voice in utterance of my name. "Granddaddy, I miss you" I can hear her whisper. What I wouldn't give to hear those few warm words spoken in my ear once again. It has been a long time now ‒ too long to recall. Where could they all have gone?

The days pass, and winter gradually makes its way into spring. It is far from the day to night alteration that I have been used to. Being a northerner, this time of year holds a heightened degree of expectation. But even in the south, the yearly warming trend tends to be chock full of intricate little eccentricities. Every place has its seasons– existing for change. Here the change is much more of a subtle variety. The grass grows a little greener on the lawns, and the thermometer climbs from warm to hot– or at the very least, warmer. Hot, perhaps, will come a little later. Something has to be saved for summer after all. Other little things change too. For instance, the varieties of birds I see about tend to differ. The ones that flew south for the winter are beginning their return northward. The time is nearly right for making my own way back as well. But as the clock turns its circles and one day bids farewell to the last, the phone never does ring, with it, bringing any news from home. Every morning I half expect Philip to knock on my apartment door or Josie to come running down. My God! I almost forgot! She won't be running down the staircase into the garden with her carefree girlish laugh to quip some quick tongued remark and give an old man a smile, perhaps making his life just a little less lonely. She won't be doing that anymore. God rest her sweet soul.

Every time I see Philip or Cloie in front of the building I mill about just a short while longer and try to make sure that they notice me there‐ just in case they somehow forgot. Perhaps it has simply slipped their minds, but someone from back home has to have called sometime. Brian and Julie couldn't have forgotten about me, surely not. I myself have tried calling them several times. By now it has become several times weekly. I will telephone my daughter's number, and always‐ every time‐ no one is home. Not once‐ not a single time, out of the entire thirteen calls I have placed‐ has anyone picked up the receiver on the other end. I don't know what could be wrong or where they might be. What if something has happened to them? I am worried, but at the same time, it is hard not to feel rejected. I am afraid that when they decided on sending me down here, they didn't plan on me coming back. When I came down here, I myself never thought I would be going back. Now, when I need them more than ever, where are they? They are no place to be found.

Margaret is now becoming more important to me than ever. I cherish the friendship and support she gives me. Her good company is my sole reliance ‐ guiding me along the dark passage I now tread. The last while has been very trying for me.   Sometimes, when I think about things, I find it hard not to fall down and cry.   I have taken care of so many. Now, these days, I am in need of someone to take care of me– someone to listen as I make my heart light, to comfort and say it's alright and whisper goodnight as I turn out the light.   I need Margy.   I have found my way, and she is here for me.

Margaret and I have come to a mutual decision: we will leave the South and travel somewhere else to set up residence. We both feel in need of starting anew, and even here, where we became us, it is still too close to the past.   The past has forgotten me, and now all I wish for is to do the same.   I want to forget too.

I am financially secure enough to enable the two of us to live a very comfortable life together. We aren't sure where we will eventually settle down.   We haven't yet made up our minds about which exact area or country.   We think it best to travel around a little first before reaching a decision.   The world is a big place– a place where you can easily find yourself lost if you are not careful.

I think about marriage.   I think about it a lot. I have never imagined myself as the sort of man who would live with a woman without being united by law and by church.   I believe the institution of marriage to be a sacred union that holds great importance in the building and maintaining of our civilization. Yet I also feel that this institution can be wasted on some people at certain points in their lives. I think it important for a young couple to be married if starting a family but not for someone of my age who is just looking for one last chance at happiness. Two failed marriages lie behind Margaret; she no longer stands in need of being married. I've had my happy marriage, built my family, and done my duty; marriage has no further business with me.   Margaret agrees: we are both free to live out the remainder of our lives as we see fit, and if that happens to include taking sanctuary in one another's company, then so be it. It is the best solution, suitable to us both.

The time is drawing near for us to leave the Yellow Moon apartments and the town of Bronsfield. Margaret asks if I wish to go home again to see my family. It will be a chance to say goodbye for what could be the last time. I want that very badly. I want to make sure that they are alright, to hold my little girl in my arms once more, and to hear the echo of her voice if only just for a whisper at a time. I would love nothing greater than to see them there again, but it doesn't matter how much I want it to happen: I know it is best to stay away. They have made it all too clear. I am no longer to be a part of their lives. Sad as it is, we have already said all our goodbyes. That is the way it has to be, for the sake of them and for the sake of me.

The night before we are to make our departure Margaret and I are invited over to Philip and Cloie's apartment for a meal. Rex Targent is a guest of theirs on this night as well. I can't help but notice that Rex and Philip have been spending a lot more time together lately. It seems as though they are becoming quite good friends. Maybe they have been all along. Cloie seems content, though. We all do. In each our own way, it is good to see us moving on with our lives. Earlier in the day Rex and Philip went fishing. We are having steaks for dinner. It is proving to be quite the good evening out. Philip remarks on it best when he happens to state "how remarkable it truly is that you are leaving this building, Georgia, and the South all under such good circumstances, how it is really kind of nice."

This evening passes into a thickening fog of memory, and a short while after we leave the South behind for good.

I never thought that I would enjoy traveling until I set forth and took engagement within the activity itself. Now I welcome each changing day with a smile. Granted, it is taking some time for me to become accustomed to the process at hand. Gradually, though, always within time, as with everything, I will become used to the general notion behind it all, and I will try to make the most of it. That is all I have ever tried to do, and I believe I have succeeded.

Southern city blues,
I know just what you're going through:
I've been trying hard to remember
Charleston…
Charleston…
Charleston…
Charleston.

Memories of you all dressed in blue….
And I kissed your neck,
and I held your hand,
and I'd do it all over again.

We're on a river
floating into shades of wanting.
We are flowing east towards the ocean
where our hearts will meet.
I'm looking at you like in a dream—
so haunting.
I lean over and gently kiss you.
Your lips are soft.
I hold your hand.
You tell me I am just the kind of man that
you've been wanting,
and I become yours forever…,
and I become yours forever.

Grey is the colour of the scenery lost on
levels in my mind.

I wish that I'd been given more time to
dream you constantly.
Then you would be with me, by my side-
the place I save for you
when the time has come when you reside.
Then we shall stay this way forever…
forever.

As the days in May, which are so perfect…
the flowers so rich in luster…
they compliment the sky
like a carpet on the floor
just a step inside heaven's door
in Charleston…
Charleston.
In Charleston…
Charleston…
Charleston.

Growing old worries me so much.
Fading memories I keep losing….
What makes my life worthwhile living
I cannot touch.
Don't want to forget you….
I don't want to forget you.

All the rivers flowing south….
You've got such a pretty mouth-
good for kissing.
My heart keeps missing beat after beat

when I'm close to you.
It's like a dream coming true.

Heaven's door has been opened.
I walk on through.
I'm floating down a river.
I'm in a boat with you.
You lean over and you whisper.
You whisper….
I can't hear you.
I can't hear you.
I can't hear you.
I can't hear you.

Southern city blues….
Southern city blues,
I know just what you're going through:
I've been trying hard to remember
Charleston…
Charleston…
Charleston…
Charleston…
Charleston…
Charleston.

Southern city blues….
Southern city blues in Charleston…
Charleston.
In Charleston…
Charleston.

38379536R00142